# The Last Affair

Eddie Crooks

© 2019 Eddie Crooks. All rights reserved

ISBN 978-0-244-51532-4

Publisher LULU.com

http//www.lulu.com/spotlight/edmin727

*Dedicated to the Memory*

*of*

*Wilhelmina (Min) Crooks*

*1935 - 2018*

# CONTENTS

|  |  |  |
|---|---|---|
|  | Foreword |  |
| Chapter 1 | A Letter of Intent | 9 |
| Chapter 2 | The First Liaison | 23 |
| Chapter 3 | Time to Reflect | 37 |
| Chapter 4 | Family Fortunes | 49 |
| Chapter 5 | Banishing the Demons | 59 |
| Chapter 6 | A Blossoming Relationship | 71 |
| Chapter 7 | A Cunning Plan | 79 |
| Chapter 8 | A Cottage in the Highlands | 89 |
| Chapter 9 | An Unwelcomed Call | 103 |
| Chapter 10 | A Family Crisis | 111 |
| Chapter 11 | His Father's Son | 125 |
| Chapter 12 | A Daughter's blessing | 131 |
| Chapter 13 | Come Back to Sorrento | 141 |
| Chapter 14 | To Be or Not to Be | 153 |
| Chapter 15 | Decision Time | 161 |
| Chapter 16 | The Sands of Time | 169 |
| Chapter 17 | The Last Reunion | 177 |
|  | The Poem | 185 |

# FOREWARD

The Last Affair is a modern story where facts are emerged into fiction. The story has three main characters, Clair, David and Elizabeth. Clair's story is factual. It is an account of her latter years suffering from dementia. This is an illness which our society has classified as a social care matter rather than a general health concern. This lack of clarity is covered in her story.

The story of David and Elizabeth is fictional. It relates to how they come together in the aftermath of a personal tragedy. A mutual attraction develops between them, inhibited by the restraint of social norms. This creates an initial barrier that could end their friendship. But their love for each other overcomes this. Their relationship grows and a twilight love affair blossoms. As they become closer their affection becomes open and subject to scrutiny. Gossip, jealousy and covert hostility put the relationship under strain. Concern for individual family matters provide a further restraint to test the strength of their relationship.

# Chapter One

## A Letter of Intent

David walked slowly up the stairs of his empty house. It was the end of three sad days and he felt very lonely. He opened his bedroom door, suppressing an inner tear as he approached his empty bed. His daughter and family had left and were on their way home. Now he was alone having attended to the rituals of his wife's funeral.

Two weeks earlier his wife Clare, finally succumbed to her dreadful illness. For four long years he had witnessed her anguish and nursed her pain as dementia slowly destroyed her brain and then in the latter weeks it destroyed the essential life giving functions of her body. He was still haunted by the formalities of her funeral. The finality of the cremation service as her coffin slowly disappeared from sight had filled him with an anguish that had been difficult to contain. The gathering of family and friends after the service offered some comfort, a sense of relief and an acceptance of the inevitability of his new life.

But now he was alone sitting on the bed that he and Clare had shared for nearly forty years. They had missed celebrating their anniversary by a few weeks because of her premature death. As he prepared for bed he took one long look around the bedroom searching for some comfort from the photographs on the dressing table and any personal objects that might retain some link with the memory of his wife. David lay back in bed, switched off the bedside lamp. In the darkness for the first time his eyes filled with an unsuppressed tear.

The days that followed were taken up by all the formalities of attending to Clare's affairs. For the time being he felt he was establishing some normality and usefulness in his life. He changed their joint bank account, cancelled her pension and contacted all the other agencies that were part of his wife's life. He was surprised at how well some responded to his calls. He found most had dedicated staff trained to deal with bereavement. The paperwork soon mounted up and so far he had managed to cope without outside help. But now the contents of the will had to be dealt with and the mysteries of probate and property title deeds compelled him to put these matters into the hands of his solicitor.

Dealing with all the paperwork helped to relieve some of the grief that overtook him at quiet times. But it became more distressing as he attended to Clare's personal belongings. Item after item revived memories and made it difficult for him to decide what to do. Clothing was packed up for collection. But personal pieces of jewellery, memories of their life together and household goods of no further use awaited some decision on disposal.

As the weeks passed, David hid his grief from view. This was made easier by the awkwardness of others and their avoidance of any meaningful questions about the death of his wife and the affect upon him. The usual question asking, 'How are you doing?' was answered by his usual response, 'Fine, I'm doing okay.'

A month had passed since Clare's death. David sat alone in his lounge. Now he knew the meaning of loneliness. His detached house was large, too large for his needs. But he was very reluctant to think of leaving to a more suitable place. During their time here it had been a happy home. Memories were all around him, memories that he still cherished. They spoke to him about Clare and the happiness and the sadness they shared together. Now, there were times, days in fact, when he spoke to no one and this feeling of being alone and the isolation was leading him down a slow path to depression.

This depression was despite his attempts to return to the normality of the outside social activities he had been forced to give up, to take care of his ailing wife. As he sat alone in his chair he was now aware that his place in society was that of a widower and no matter how much outside contacts he had, ultimately his status quo was that of a lonely old man.

Three months had now passed. His wife's estate was being slowly settled but his solicitor seemed to be taking a long time to deal with remaining matters. He collected his morning post and his newspaper, noting the date. It was the day the Parkview Social Club held its monthly meeting. He hesitated for a moment and thought it would be a good opportunity to attend and perhaps get out of the house. Both he and Clare had been regular members up until a few years ago when her health seriously deteriorated.

Clare had been more active in the club activities than him, so he was a little apprehensive as he entered the meeting room. The hall was busy and as he paid his dues, he looked around for a familiar contact. At the far end he saw one of his old golf companions sitting with his wife and another couple. He quickly passed the tables occupied mainly by the ladies, giving brief acknowledgements on the way.

'May I join you?' he asked,

'Of course!' he replied.

David was introduced to the other couple. After a few moments of conversation he was happy to leave the two couples to talk amongst them selves. He settled back to listen to the lecture. The subject was of no real interest to him so he found it difficult to concentrate. So he relaxed and looked around the room noting a few married couples but mainly groups of ladies. Most were strangers who had joined the club during his absence, but one or two familiar faces remained. The lecture finished and the room filled with the babble of conversation. He waited for a cup of coffee and then chose the moment to make an early departure with a less than convincing excuse and set off home. He came away with mixed feelings about the day, but now it was time to think about his evening meal.

It was early evening and he was busy in his kitchen preparing his meal. Clare was the provider of meals during there time together and he had never seen the need to do more in the kitchen than the statutory washing up after their meals. As her illness progressed she gradually lost the ability to do these things and he had to provide for their needs. During this time he had to rely greatly on convenient ready meals from his local supermarket. Their simple instruction giving cooking time and temperature helped to sustain their needs. This limited skill in the kitchen remained with him and was sufficient to maintain his independence. He stood patiently in front of the cooker waiting for the timer to reach its final setting when the telephone rang. The unexpected noise startled him. It was too early for a family call and other calls were few and far between. He picked up the receiver.

'Hello,' he greeted the unknown caller.

'Hello David, this is Elizabeth here;' came a reply.

David hesitated, he wasn't sure who she was and paused for a moment to let her explain. She sensed his caution and quickly responded.

'It's Elizabeth Stewart, one of Clair's friends. I saw you at the meeting this afternoon, didn't get a chance to speak to you.'

'Ah yes; I remember now.' came his tentative reply.

She quickly responded, 'When you left the meeting this afternoon we wondered how you were coping, I said I would ring you this evening. We all miss Clare so it must be especially hard for you.'

'That was kind of you;' he replied and then he gave his usual response. 'I am coping well, no problems really;' which he knew was not the whole truth.

David listened patiently as she continued with her call. There was something very interesting in the lilt of her voice. It was an attractive voice, a caring voice.

'It was kind of you to call, I will make a point of speaking to you at the next meeting;' said David.

'That would be lovely, but if I can be of any help in the meantime give me a call;' came her reply as she ended her call. Too late! David realised he had not asked for her telephone number and cursed quietly for being so slow. Then he realised that the details would likely be in Clare's old address book, and there it was much to his delight. But then he wondered why he was so interested in that information and why she seemed so interested in him.

Elizabeth replaced the receiver, she was pleased that she decided to call David and pleased that he seemed pleased with her unsolicited call. She hadn't been completely truthful about her reason. She had not discussed this with her friends during the club meeting. She first noted his arrival and could see how uneasy he was. When he left at the end of the meeting there was a fleeting glance of recognition that raised her interest. So it was enough that she understood his position and might appreciate her call.

She knew from her own experience how David might be coping with the difficulties of bereavement. Elizabeth was in her early sixties when her husband died a few years earlier. She understood the problems of being a grieving widow and the difficulties of finding a new place in society. Elizabeth had coped well with her own bereavement at the time. Her grief had been kept in check. Outwardly, her positive outlook and personality led to an active way of life. She took on responsibilities in the social club and developed new friendships with some ease.

The attraction that David picked up during their conversation was apparent in Elizabeth's personality. Her hair was grey with blond twinges. She had an attractive face that still retained essential signs of the beauty she possessed in her younger years. Her voice was soft but lively and outwardly she was self assured and comfortable in company.

Elizabeth and her late husband knew David and Clare over a number of years. They were acquaintances, certainly not close friends but they shared many happy occasions as members of their club. Social evenings, day trips and the occasional club holiday brought them into contact from time to time.

The loneliness of being a widow was something she occasionally experienced at home in her neat flat. Beneath her social demeanour there lay a nagging uncertainty about the future and what lay in store for her. She could see and feel the inevitable processes of ageing affecting her looks and her body. Inner feelings and outward pains stalked her being. Sometimes it was a struggle for her to maintain her outward persona. In these moments of doubt she felt anxious and depressed. It was evident to her that her personal fears for the future could best be served by sharing them possibly in partnership with someone else. But how could that be and by whom?

It was with these thoughts in mind that she had tentatively picked up the phone to speak to David. Having spoken to him she was now conscious of a certain attraction and a hope that it would be shared by him. Quickly, she banished the thought.

'David was still in grief at the loss of his wife and it was no time for her to interfere in his affairs;' she thought.

Time passed since Elizabeth's brief call. There was no reason for them to be in regular contact. David's personal affairs and his limited social life were far removed from that of Elizabeth. She led an active social life. She lived in a nice flat with good neighbours and regularly attended her local church. Her only regret was the absence of her family. She missed her son, his wife and her grandson Stephen. But she reasoned they had their own lives to live and she was content with hers.

Circumstances might change in the future. But for the time being these were concerns that only troubled her after a bad day when her insecurity took command. So, meetings between David and Elizabeth were few and far between. They met at club meetings and occasionally spoke on the phone when necessary. However a mutual sense of caution prevented more personal contact.

Six months had now passed and David had a personal problem or at least an excuse to involve Elizabeth. His late wife's wardrobe had been emptied and despatched to the local charity shop. Ornaments and other household goods that Clare had valued but were of no further interest to him had been sold or given away. But what should he do about her jewellery? These items were really personal and memories of special shared occasions. Some were kept by his daughter but he was left with too much to handle on his own.

So he spoke to Elizabeth on the phone. She seemed interested to discuss his problem and gave helpful advice. He hoped that she might offer to visit him to see the articles, but no such offer came. They talked casually about other matters, their common interests and more personal talk about their respective families. But he hoped that there could be a more personal and mutual relationship beyond the occasional telephone call.

David was now feeling very confused about this distant and infrequent relationship he had with Elizabeth. When they spoke on the phone, her voice, which so attracted him from the beginning, seemed to be sending coded messages he was finding difficult to interpret. He wished he could have a more intimate face to face conversation with her, and not the restrictions of the phone which was a barrier that inhibited meaningful contact. He was beginning to feel the need for a more intimate companionship with Elizabeth. But their telephone conversations never quite gave him that invitation.

Being a widower placed limitations on his life. He wondered how long the grieving process should last for his late wife, and what would be the consequences if that was seen to end too soon. He consoled himself by knowing that grief for his wife started years before she died. Could sharing a visit to a theatre or attending some local event or even sharing a walk in a park be possible without embarrassment or gossip? But, of greater importance, he wondered about Elizabeth's feelings. She was always friendly without giving any hint of interest other than the coded messages that were being hopelessly misinterpreted by him.

David was at home casually thumbing through the pages of the local news paper. He noticed a theatre advert for a forthcoming musical show. South Pacific was a favourite of his and he thought about going. He didn't care to go on his own, and thought that perhaps he could invite Elizabeth to accompany him. It seemed a good idea, not only good company but an opportunity to make progress in their distant and frustrating relationship. His immediate thought was to pick up the phone, but he paused. What if she refused and gave some feeble excuse. What if she reacted badly suggesting it would embarrass her to be seen with a man whose wife had only recently passed away.

His negative thoughts overpowered his good intentions and he abandoned any thought of making such a decisive call. A call that perhaps could unlock all the frustration he was feeling. This frustration was not going to subside, he realised, so he had to do something to bring matters to a head. Instinctively he knew it would be difficult to raise these delicate matters on the phone. He feared his thoughts would be confused and he would not find the right words to make his case. Most importantly he felt he would be unable to judge her reactions to what he needed to say. Finally he came to a decision. He would write a letter. 'Was this a coward's way out?' he wondered. It would be a short letter perhaps, to thank her for helping him through difficult times. But it would make clear his affection for her and the hope of a more meaningful relationship.

David faced his blank sheet of paper and picked up his pen. He wondered where to start. It wasn't easy to transfer his confused thoughts into words. After a few failed attempts he finished the letter. He was satisfied that it was brief and not too serious, but it conveyed his feelings adequately enough. He folded the page neatly and placed it in the envelope. He carefully wrote her address in his best handwriting and sealed the envelope. He thought about delivering it by hand but decided it would be best to send it by post.

Reflecting now on what he was doing made him realise that his letter would make or break any possibility of his hopes. The letter gave the initiative to Elizabeth who would now set their future. The one consolation he saw in her rejection was that he would know finally where he stood and they could get on with their lives following different paths.

David approached the post box holding the letter in his hand. He wondered if he was doing the right thing. This could go terribly wrong if he had misread the signs. He paused for a moment. The letter was balanced between his finger tips and the lip of the post box. Finally, he let it go and it fell gently beyond his reach. It was gone, he could not bring it back and he could not change any of the consequences when it was delivered to its destination. David realised that now he would have to wait before he would know what these consequences were.

The next few days passed very slowly. He worked out when the letter might be delivered, possibly no more than two days. He allowed another day for her to read the letter and reply. His assumption was that he would know her response within these three days. But that day passed and so it went on for a full week. He was left with the disappointing conclusion that she read the letter and for what ever reason she rejected his overture. By now he was despondent and regretted ever thinking that writing a letter was a good idea.

*David Fulton was born and lived in the sea side town of Southport for the past seventy two years. When his parents passed away twenty five years ago he inherited the family home. It was a large detached house close to the centre of the town. His late wife Clare and his only daughter Julie shared a house that was too large for their needs, but it was a comfortable property and they were very happy. Julie trained as a nurse at the local hospital and then left to take up a post in Newcastle. There she met a local lad, they got married and now had twins, two girls called Susan and Jane. David retired eight years ago with a good pension and savings. So he and Clare had planned to move to a smaller property and enjoy their retirement years. But, Clare's long illness changed all their plans. Now he was left alone in a home full of lifelong memories that provided little comfort for his lone existence.*

# Chapter Two

## The First Liaison

It was late in the evening when Elizabeth returned home. She paid for the taxi from the station and struggled up the driveway with her luggage. Opening the door to the block of flats, she checked her post box and collected the contents stuffing them carelessly into her shoulder bag. The following morning she woke up late, having had a poor night's sleep. Her journey had been very stressful but that did not account for the headache that kept her awake during the night. She finished her light breakfast before remembering the unread post still in her bag. The mail was mostly advertising leaflets which were disposed of straight away. Two brown envelopes were clearly official business to be read later. But the white envelope caught her attention. The address was written in a clear steady script and she noted that there was no post code.

'It must be from a stranger.' she thought.

She opened the envelope neatly with her breakfast knife and unfolded the single sheet of paper. It was written in the same clear handwriting as the envelope and she was surprised to see that it came from David.

'Why was he sending her a letter?' she wondered.
The date at the top of the letter showed that it had been written two days before she left to visit her son in London. She began to read the letter and her initial reaction sent her emotions into a confused flurry. He was clearly laying his cards on the table and she was lost for words.

'The Old Fool!' she exclaimed under her breath. 'It's a damned love letter.' The consequences of David's letter slowly dawned on her as she read it for a second time. But suddenly the date on the letter caused her to panic. He had written ten days ago and there was no way for him to know she was away. She wondered what he would be thinking of her for not at least acknowledging that his letter had arrived. Her thoughts turned to a more serious matter. The letter now cleared an uncertainty that made all things possible. David's bereavement was no longer an impediment to a closer relationship. But she reasoned that this might not be so simple for others to accept if their friendship became more open. However, any guilt she felt about David's position had now gone. She folded the letter, placed it in the envelope and put it in a safe place. Her immediate thought was to speak to David straight away to apologise and explain the delay in responding to his letter. A feeling of deep pleasure embraced her as the artificial barriers to a new relationship began to vanish.

Elizabeth picked up her phone and dialled David's home number. It rang for quite a time before the call was answered and she began to feel nervous.

'Hello?'

'David, it's me;' she paused to regain her composure.

'Thank you for your letter,' she continued but before she could say another word, David interrupted her.

Oh, thank goodness you called;' he replied. 'If the letter has upset you I hope you will forgive me. When you didn't phone I felt I couldn't phone you so, I am really sorry and feel a damned idiot.'

'It's okay David I've been away over the last week in London visiting my son.' she explained.

'I loved your letter David.' she said reassuringly.

It was an affectionate response and David detected it in the tone of her voice. He was pleased and any doubts he held about sending the letter were now gone. From now on there would be no more coded messages for him to interpret. They talked for a while before he got round to ask an important question.

'So where do we go from her?' he asked in a light hearted sort of way. 'We have a lot to talk about now, and not just over the phone.'

'Yes.' she agreed. 'We could meet somewhere and have a chat over a cup of coffee, any suggestions?'

Before he could answer, she continued. 'I know where we could meet without being too conspicuous. I usually shop at M&S on a Friday. We could meet in the upstairs café. How about that?' she asked.

'Sounds good, I'll meet you at the front entrance, what time suits you?'

'Eleven o'clock?' she suggested.

They both agreed and replaced their receivers. David experienced a rare felling of joy and anticipation of a developing friendship.

He was too early for their meeting so he casually walked up and down Chapel Street awaiting her arrival. He saw her approaching the store and, as if by accident fabricated a casual encounter. They made there way into the store and up the escalator towards the café. A queue had formed at the self service counter so David suggested that Elizabeth should find an empty table.

'What would you like?' he asked.

'Just a coffee please, nothing else.' she replied.

He stood in the queue awaiting his turn, casually gazing at the tables to see where she was sitting.

'Next please!' brought his attention back to the girl behind the counter.

'Can I have two coffees please?'

'What kind of coffee would you like?'

He looked up at the board she was pointing to, which was displaying six different blends in two different sizes. The question confused him for a moment. He realised he should have asked her what she preferred, but it was too late now.

'Can I have ordinary coffees with milk please?'

He hoped that Elizabeth was not expecting one of the more exotic blends.

She was seated at a table by a window close to adjacent tables that were occupied. There was no possibility of any serious discussion without being overheard. So their conversation was quietly discrete. Their meeting was pleasant enough and they parted to go their own ways. David had promised to phone in the evening to arrange for another one to one meeting. He was relieved that they seemed to get on well together. There were no embarrassing silences and he felt that they had a lot in common.

Elizabeth settled down for a quiet evening in her flat. She wasn't sure when he would phone or if he would phone as promised. She switched the television on to catch her favourite nightly programme when the phone rang. She picked up the receiver and hurriedly switched off the television before it had time to warm up.

They talked for a long time. The conversation was much freer, almost flirtatious at times. David had no more thoughts of coded messages and

Elizabeth was now at ease over her concerns about David's personal situation and the propriety of their friendship. They were about to end the call, but before doing so, he had one last request.

'How about meeting again soon?'

'Yes, let's, where do you suggest?' she replied.

'Not the café, somewhere more private.' he suggested.

There was a brief pause then David made a bold suggestion.

'If you are comfortable with this invitation, why not come round to my house? I make a good cup of coffee and it's a lot quieter than the café.' She was slightly taken aback by his boldness, but the invitation had some appeal.

'Oh! This could be embarrassing, what would your neighbours think?' He detected that trace of frivolity in her reply and pressed home his suggestion.

'Don't worry about the neighbours, if they did notice you arriving they would probably think you were calling on business. I've had many callers on business over the last few years.' There was a trace of bitterness in his voice.

'I'm comfortable with that. 'I'll bring a brief case if that's alright?' David detected that wonderful cheery lilt in her voice again.

David glanced at his watch. It was ten minutes to two. Elizabeth was expected in ten minutes. He filled his coffee percolator with water and heaped four spoonfuls of coffee into the paper filter. He had spent most of the day sprucing the house up, as best he could. It reminded him of preparing for the CO's Inspection when he was in the RAF. Now she was late, which wasn't too unexpected. He went towards the window just in time to see her park her car on the opposite side of the road. He discretely watched as she got out of the car. His pulse raised just a little as she crossed the road. She was neatly dressed in a two piece suit and sure enough she was carrying a brief case. He went to the front door and opened it before she had a chance to ring the bell. He gave her a friendly embrace and invited her into his house. She handed over her brief case and the two of them laughed at the absurdity of her subterfuge. They both laughed in a way that relieved any awkwardness or tension that could have occurred with this liaison. He ushered her into his sitting room and invited her to take a seat. He sat opposite and broke the initial silence.

'I'm glad you agreed to come, I'm really pleased to see you.'

She smiled at him 'It's my pleasure, honestly,'

She looked around the room noting the family photographs and the framed photograph of his late wife. For a moment she felt uneasy thinking that Clare might be looking down disapproving her intrusion into David's life. She quickly recovered her composure.

'Is that your daughter and the family?

David was happy to talk about the pictures. It was a good opening for getting to know each other. He asked her about her son and what he did in London. She enthusiastically relayed all the details of her family.

The faint aroma of coffee coming from the kitchen suddenly alerted him. He apologised for his poor hospitality and went into the kitchen to dispense two cups of coffee from the percolator and remove the covering from the plateful of biscuits. Now with all the formalities over, they settled down and talked for a long time, exchanging details of their separate lives. Then Elizabeth changed the subject.

'You know David, your letter came as a great shock;' she paused to find the right words.

'It was very sweet, honestly it was like a love letter.'
She looked at him and felt a slight blush on her cheeks.

'Whatever made you want to write a letter?' she asked.

David laughed, 'It's been a very long time since I wrote anything like that.'

He thought for a moment and continued, 'When I was a teenager we used to meet girls on a Saturday night at the local dance hall. That was the place to 'click' as we used to call it. Anyway I did click with a girl called Moira. We dated for a couple of months even got invited for tea to meet the parents. So it was getting a bit serious. Out of the blue, she called it off for no obvious reason. I must have been a bit love sick. So I wrote her a letter, it wasn't exactly a letter it was a soppy poem.'

'Did you send it?' she asked'

'No.' he replied. 'In fact I think I still have it somewhere.'

'Can you get it? I would love to read it.'

'Maybe one day I'll find it for you.'

'You really are an old romantic!' she cried.

He looked at her and said. 'Maybe I was then, but not now. That was written a long long time ago.'

'You still are a romantic, and I have the letter to prove it!' she exclaimed.

He returned to his story. 'Anyway, I did find out the reason she dropped me. Her parents put pressure on her to give me up because we were of different religions.'

'Really?' She looked surprised.

'Yes it's true, in those days mixed marriages were taboo. Not like today when anything goes!'

Elizabeth glanced at her watch, they had been chatting for nearly two hours. It was time to go home. David sensed that enough had been said for their first meeting but was still hoping she could stay for a while longer. So he asked her if she would like to have a look around his house. She was too polite to say no, but she was also too curious to refuse. So David led her into the dining room and then the adjoining sun lounge where she admired the view of the garden.

'What a lovely view. You must spend a lot of time in here?'

David nodded, appreciative of her warm reaction. They then made there way from the hall into the kitchen. She again made appreciative remarks but silently thought it was a little dated and could benefit from a modern makeover. Having surveyed all that was to be seen downstairs, they returned to the hall and he pointed the way to the upper floor. When they reached the top of the stairs she noticed the five doors.

'Gosh this is a really big house. How do you manage here all on your own?'

'It's not too much of a problem, it keeps me fit climbing up and down these damned stairs' he replied as he opened the nearest door.

'This is the guest's bedroom. It's not used so much these days.'
She took a quick look, not wishing to be seen to be too inquisitive. Another door opened into a smaller brightly decorated bedroom. He commented that this was Julie's bedroom before she left to get married. The third door stayed closed and he apologised saying it was full of stuff he needed to get rid of.

They moved to the fourth door.

'This is my bedroom;' he said, standing to one side to allow Elizabeth to enter.

She felt a slight embarrassment, 'I'm not used to entering an unattached man's bedroom.' she thought.

'This is a lovely room David,' she said as she looked around while avoiding paying too much attention to the king size bed. She also noted that the room was bare of ornaments or the usual things to be found on a ladies dressing table.

Suddenly and without much thought she said,

'It's very nice but it needs a woman's touch.'
She felt like biting her tongue off. 'What a stupid thing to say!' she thought. She continued to inwardly scold herself. 'If he is offended then I could be very embarrassed if he asks me the obvious question.'

David heard her comment, but he was wise enough not to pursue the opportunity so her panic moment passed by. But he was shrewd enough to note it as another coded message to be deciphered at another time. The tour of the house was now finished and they stood in the hall ready for her departure. 'Thanks for coming, I hope it will not be the last time.' he said.

'I would love to come again, it was a nice day so thank you.' she replied.

David gave her a departing embrace that was more meaningful than before. He briefly kissed her cheek and she thrilled at the closeness between them. He picked up her brief case and handed it to her.

'Don't bring that next time!'

She laughed acknowledging the silliness of it all.

Elizabeth crossed the road towards her car. She took a deep breath of the late afternoon air and recollected how warm and still, almost stuffy it was in the house.

'Definitely needs a woman's touch' she thought again as she sat herself down in the car and paused for a moment. She could feel the beginning of another headache coming on so she needed to get home. When she arrived home she took a tablet prescribed by her doctor to relieve her recurring headaches. It had been a pleasant but emotionally stressful day. Now she was tired and ready for an early bedtime. As she pulled her duvet cover up to her chin she thought of David.

'I wonder if he is tucked up in his king size bed?' She smiled inwardly,

'I wonder if it's as comfortable as it appears?'

Then she turned and put out her bedside lamp. She rested on her pillow, with happy thoughts lulling her to sleep.

When she wakened the following morning she knew she had been dreaming, but she had no recollection of the details. All she knew was that she was still thinking about David. But now she had other things to attend to in preparation for the new day and her shower was first on the list. The steady downpour of warm water revitalised her body and soothed away the remnants of last evening's headache. She turned the shower off stepped out of the cubical, dried herself and attended to her usual morning routine. Her bath towel was securely held around her chest as she faced the mirror in her bedroom. She allowed the towel to drop away and looked in the mirror. She wasn't displeased at her naked body. Turning from side to side, she contented herself, concluding she was still in good shape. She lingered looking in the mirror recalling thoughts that had lain dormant for a long time, certainly since before she became a widow.

Elizabeth Stewart was a born and bread Londoner. Her late husband was a senior civil servant and they lived in Essex with their young son Michael. She was a primary school teacher. They were settled there and very happy until her husband was promoted and compelled to move to a new location in Liverpool. This created family problems. Liverpool was not an attractive proposition and she was upset because her son had just received a grant to attend a private boarding school. However, they had to move and they chose to stay in Southport because of its easy access into Liverpool. The difference in house prices allowed them to buy a new property with a spectacular view over the Mersey Estuary. Then tragedy struck when her husband died suddenly and Elizabeth was left alone in their home. Her financial position changed dramatically and she was forced to sell her house and move into a flat. During her latter years she made new friends she was socially active and was now content with her life.

## Chapter Three

## Time to Reflect

The anniversary of Clare's passing would soon be upon David. Three months had gone by since he became attached to Elizabeth. During that time they were intent on respecting Clare's memory and protecting family feelings concerning their relationship. From the start they agreed that they would keep a low profile away from public scrutiny. Southport is a comparatively small seaside town so it was difficult to be discrete. A distinctive feature of the town is Lord Street, a broad tree lined boulevard that is said to have inspired the design of the Champs Elysee in Paris. This was a pleasant place to walk. Mingling with the many visitors made it easy for them to go unnoticed. They also found the towns two parks, the Botanic Gardens and Hesketh Park were places where they could stroll and talk without concern. All these places reflected the towns faded Victorian elegance.

They took special care to arrange their meetings to be as private as possible until they could judge when the time would be right to be open about this, but certainly it would not be before the anniversary of Clare's death. So far they had been reasonably successful in keeping a low profile, but occasionally they were exposed to casual observation and comment. On one occasion at their club meeting David had been overtly chatty with her as she sat with her friends. This caused a few inquisitive comments amongst the ladies which Elizabeth dismissed as 'stuff and nonsense.'

They did meet regularly and discretely. Elizabeth visited his home on a number of occasions. They devised a way of going to the local Vue Cinema. David ordered tickets in advance. They parked their cars separately in the Ocean Plaza car park and met up in the foyer. The cinema was a perfect place where they could enjoy each others company. On one occasion he thought about holding hands, but soon discovered that modern day cinema seats with their wide arm rests and the integrated drinks holder made that objective near impossible. So they resorted to occasional glances and exchange of sweets as the next best thing. Elizabeth's frequent visits to the house were attracting neighbourly comment but this did not worry David at all. He felt that most of his neighbours kept their distance at his most lonely times and now it was none of their business.

The anniversary was now two weeks away. David's daughter Julie and husband James and their children were coming to stay with him over the period. Elizabeth intended to keep her distance while they were there. So, she looked forward to visiting David one more time before they arrived. A doctor's appointment prevented the usual afternoon visit so it was arranged for her to call that evening. She parked her car outside the house and was greeted in the usual manner by David. Without any formality she settled herself in the lounge. The television was on and they both watched the evening news. When it finished he brought in two mugs of tea and switched the TV off.

David knew that she was worried about her recurring headaches and that was why she had the appointment with her doctor.

'What did the doctor have to say about your headaches?'
She didn't really want to talk about that and passed it over quickly.
'He does not think it is too much of a problem.' she replied and added, 'So it's a case of keep on taking the tablets.'
She laughed and quickly changed the subject to talk about David.

Elizabeth felt from early on in their relationship that the death of his wife hurt him more than he was prepared to let on. Something troubled him, and she was concerned enough that he needed help. With the approaching anniversary the time was right to see if she could free him from his inner demons.

'David, can I ask you something very personal?
'I mean about how you are coping with the loss of Claire, it's nearly a year now and you hardly talk about your feelings.'
He was tempted to dismiss her question with his usual non-committal reply when he paused. For the first time he knew this was a genuine question and he was ready to answer.

'To be perfectly frank, the thought of Claire and the thought of what she went through in the last years of her life haunt me with sadness and guilt.'

She was surprised at his answer to her question and his mention of guilt. She was aware of enough statements from survivors of tragedies to realise this was a sign of a special kind of stress.

'Please, carry on. Tell me all about what is worrying you.'
She could see the apprehension in his eyes and added,
'Take your time darling.'
He sat back in his chair, took a deep breath and began.
'It goes back a long time, probably six or seven years. One early morning, I was wakened to find Clare out of bed and in a really bad way. She was hysterical and screaming, 'I've lost my breasts.' I couldn't calm her down. She was getting worse so I dialled 999. She was taken off to the hospital to A&E. By the time I got to the hospital she was sitting up in the bed - as bright as a button.'
He paused to look at Elizabeth before continuing.
'You can imagine how much of a relief that was. They said she had suffered some form of shock and it was a reaction to a high level of anxiety.'

Elizabeth asked, 'What did she mean about her breasts?'
'Well it was true in a way. Her breasts had lost their firmness and were,' he hesitated, 'well sort of flat. I had put it down to a sort of

ageing thing. Maybe I should have been more understanding at the time.'

He was now more relaxed knowing that Elizabeth was prepared to listen to him. So he continued.

'The anxiety was the problem so we made an appointment with her doctor. He had the report from the hospital and suggested an appointment at a clinic where they specialised in psychiatric problems. During the first appointment she had a number of memory tests which went reasonably well, except she had difficulty in copying simple shapes like a square with a triangle on top that looked like a house.'

'The clinic set up a number of appointments where she did similar tests with the same results. They eventually said that she was suffering from Pre-Cognitive Deficiency. I remember asking what that meant and was told it could be the early signs of dementia.'

'Our final visit to the clinic was very brief. We sat in the consultant's office and waited while she studied Claire's file. In a matter of fact way she looked at me, not Clare, and said that Clare was suffering from vascular dementia. The consultant gave me some leaflets and booklets to explain the disease then still looking at me she said there was no need for further appointments and Claire's file was going back to her doctor.'

'We sat in the car afterwards and I remember Clare burst into tears. Looking back now, I don't think I showed her enough sympathy or understanding - how could I know her inner thoughts at that news. Anyway, that's something I regret now.'

He paused to look at Elizabeth and he was reassured and continued.

'For a while we coped reasonably well although her condition was more noticeable and social occasions became difficult. When we were out for a meal with friends she would take an age to finish her food. It became embarrassing having the others wait for her. It was only a matter of time before things got worse.'

Elizabeth interrupted him. 'Surely they would have understood Clare's position. It's a pity you felt the need to withdraw as you said.'

'It wasn't that simple' he replied.

'It wasn't just her mind that was being affected. It was affecting her body in more serious ways.' He went on to explain.

'We were going on a holiday with the club to Scarborough. Do you remember it? Three weeks before we were due to leave, Clare had another panic attack. This was more serious and to my shame I was angry and frustrated. Anyway, I got her doctor to call because she couldn't get out of bed. She needed to go to hospital. So we packed a bag on his advice and reported to the A&E Department. They carried out their checks and she was admitted to a ward. That was on a Thursday and I remember she was in good spirits by the time I left. I spoke to the duty doctor who said they planned to carry out tests. This involved a scan which they hoped to do on the Friday, but that was subject to availability of the equipment.'

'So what happened next?'

'Nothing!' he replied.

'The scan was cancelled on the Friday and because they didn't do this procedure at the weekend, it was postponed to the following week, again subject to availability. Over the weekend her condition deteriorated badly. When I visited her on Sunday she was on a drip and guard rails were fitted to her bed to prevent her from falling out. Eventually she had a CT and an MRI scan that ruled out a mini stroke, but she had to stay in hospital for another two weeks. They gave her different treatments but eventually she was discharged in reasonably good health. I had to cancel the holiday of course!'

David suddenly recollected something that had slipped his mind.

'You know, Claire suffered a lot of medical problems over the years. She had a number of operations and some were not very successful. She managed to endure these calmly and get on with her life, that's the way she was before all this. But her most recent problem was severe varicose veins in both legs. It was a vanity thing and to my regret, I encouraged her to see her doctor. She was referred to the hospital and the consultant agreed to carry out the procedure. Because of the nature of her veins the consultant ruled out the more conventional procedure in favour one that involved injecting foam into the veins to block them and divert the blood flow. It was only later on that I read somewhere that one of the possible side effects of this operation was restricting blood to the brain! That was never mentioned before the operation. I still don't know if this was true or not. If it was true it was certainly relevant to someone who had been diagnosed with vascular dementia. The operation was never successful and to this day I wish I hadn't persuaded Clare to have it.'

Elizabeth could see that this was beginning to upset David and she was equally emotional listening to his story. Before he could go on she said,

'Let's have a break. I'll go and make us a cup of coffee. Just you wait there.'

With that, she was up and off into the kitchen. David sat back in his seat with a feeling of relief that he was able to talk and that Elizabeth was so willing to listen. Elizabeth returned with two mugs of coffee and they chatted about other things, but she was anxious to get him to continue his story.

'It has been really interesting listening to you. Please carry on;' she said encouragingly.

'It's good to be able to talk like this;' he replied.

'I think I said we managed to cope most of the time. Well, one thing we did together early on was our weekly shopping in the supermarket. Clare would hold on to the trolley and push it up and down the aisles.

Meanwhile I would rush around picking up the shopping. Then I had to search for her and the trolley, usually to find she was chatting to an unsuspecting and sometimes slightly annoyed shopper.'

'But that routine had its problems. She became terribly incontinent and it could happen so quickly at any time. Often I had to abandon a half full trolley to guide her to the toilet and wait for her. She took so long sometimes that it looked like I was loitering with intent!'

Elizabeth tried to suppress a smile at his predicament.

He continued, 'We got to the stage where I had to put a pair of knickers in a plastic bag in her handbag to cover emergencies. You won't believe this!' he added looking at Elizabeth.

'This went on for some time until one day a leaflet came with the post. It had the usual advertising stuff, but it also had a voucher offering a free packet of ladies incontinence pads. I think they were called 'Tena Pads'. Anyway I found the free offer in the shop. Honestly, they were marvellous, we never looked back. They made life so much simpler.'

Elizabeth laughed loudly.

'Didn't you know you could get these free on the NHS?'

'No.' he replied.

'Nobody told me, so how was I supposed to know?'

It was getting late but Elizabeth was still listening intently so David carried on with his recollections.

'If our shopping trip went well I sometimes suggested we stay for a snack or a cup of tea in the café. We would be seated at the table, quite relaxed when her eyes would go funny like. She would stare at me, but not really connecting. I learned to know that this was the start of something that is hard to describe. She seemed to lose control of her body, not in a violent way. No, she would be quite passive but unable to even hold a cup or pick up a biscuit. Stupidly, I sometimes got embarrassed, worrying about her and how she felt, because she never spoke. She became unsteady and needed to be guided out of the shop. Needless to say, our visits to the café were few and far between!'

Elizabeth's eyes were moist with tears. She tried to hide her emotions and the pity she felt for him, and for Clare. It was late evening with the last of the daylight fading into the night. David's recollections had been so intense that he forgot to draw the blinds. 'So much for keeping the neighbours in the dark!' he thought. He leaned over to hold Elizabeth's hand. 'Thank you for listening to my tales of woe. It has been good for me to get this off my chest.'

She stood up and moved towards him and held him in a comforting lingering embrace. 'I know, I know.' she whispered.
He turned, pointing to the clock. 'There is so much more to tell you, but look at the time. Maybe next time I can finish the story.'
She looked at him saying, 'Oh yes, it's so sad but so interesting. I had no idea how much you both suffered over such a long time. You must finish your story.'

He nodded in agreement. 'It's really helpful to talk about this; the bad times that still ring in my head.'

'I hope my listening has helped;' she whispered.

She laid her head on his shoulder to console him.

The faint aroma of her perfume and the warmth of the embrace were comforting. He didn't want to let her go. He wanted her to stay, but resisted the temptation of asking that question.

'Look it's getting dark, let me drive you home. We can use your car. It's no problem for me to walk home afterwards.

'No, honestly I will be fine. I'll phone you when I get home so no need to be worried.'

He escorted her down his driveway and opened the car door. He leaned down and lightly kissed her on the cheek. She drove off and he stood on the pavement until the car was out of sight. David walked up his driveway pausing to take in the night air. For the first time in many years he felt an inner peace of mind. He was grateful to Elizabeth for listening and encouraging him to ease his troubled mind. But he knew that his story was only half told and worse was to come.

# Chapter Four

## Family Fortunes

The house was alive again. David's family had arrived and the noise from his two grandchildren and the conversations with his daughter and son-in-law made him realise how lonely he was since his wife passed away. He was still missing Elizabeth's company, more so now that she was staying with her son and family in London. Elizabeth had talked about this first meeting with their families and they both wondered if it would be the right time to alert them to their new found friendship. They both agreed it was not the right time but if an opportunity arose, a gentle hint might simplify matters in the future.

Opportunities are always there and one did occur for David.

The family get together to remember Clare was a sad and fairly muted occasion. There was no gravestone to be visited or to lay flowers. His wife was cremated and her ashes were laid by David, privately at a favourite spot He had visited the location a number of times, knowing that her remains were absorbed into the soil beneath his feet. So in a way he felt that her presence was always there. It had become a place of comfort and quiet reflection.

His family returned home from a restaurant after an evening meal. It wasn't the happiest of occasions but it was respectful of Clare's memory. A few remembrance cards on display attracted Julie's attention. She picked one up to read,

'It's kind of people to remember Mum. A year is a long time!' she added.

'It has been a long time for you too Dad. How do you manage here on your own?

I keep asking you to move nearer to us!'

Her husband gave her a glance and she recognised its significance. He was not so keen on that idea, it had consequences. Ignoring this visual warning she carried on. You are missing out on being a grandfather to Susan and Jane and they miss you too. I don't like you being up here on your own.'

'I am not alone up here. I have lots of friends and I am getting back into doing things I gave up when your Mum was ill.'

This was the opportunity he discussed with Elizabeth,

'I have a lady friend that has been very helpful!' The tone of his voice was not quite as humorous as he hoped.

This was quite a shock for Julie, but she managed to contain her initial reaction.

'Dad! What do you mean by a lady friend?'

'It's not what you might be thinking! We have known each other for years. She was a friend of your Mum and we sometimes meet at the social club. We just talk, nothing more than that!'

Julie was confused. Inwardly she had the natural feeling of a daughter that her father was being disrespectful to the memory of her mother. But on the other hand she was pleased that there could be something in his life that was good for him.'

'What is her name?' she asked.

'Elizabeth;' he replied.

'I will have to keep an eye on you.' She said as she walked over to her father and gave him a knowing embrace.

'Good for you Pop!' was the immediate response from James.

The conversation was abruptly terminated by the grand children as they burst into the room. David was quietly pleased. The first seeds of the truth had been well and truly planted.

Elizabeth's visit to her son was arranged at short notice. She thought it was best if she was not around to distract David and his family at a sensitive time. Unfortunately the visit proved to be inconvenient for Michael her son. Although she loved her son and her grandchild, there were times when her visits were stressful. She was not on best terms with Margaret, her daughter in law. They had not got on well from the start and their remained a coolness which surfaced from time to time after a misspoken word or action. Elizabeth had planned to stay for a week but was persuaded to leave a day early because they would be away at some function or other. Elizabeth was anxious to let David know of the change of plan and also to find out how he was coping with his family and the remembrance of his late wife. She asked Michael if she could use the house phone. He agreed and she went into the hall, picked up the phone and called David's number.

'David, darling it's me;' she said in a quiet voice.

'How are you getting on?' she listened to his reply and responded.

'Yes I'm fine, having a nice time here, but I really miss you.'

She looked around to make sure no one was in sight.

'I am coming home early on Friday. My train arrives at three thirty in the afternoon.'

She listened again.

'No, no there's no need to pick me up I will get a taxi.' she paused.

'Alright if you insist, see you at the station.'

'I miss you too darling, can't wait to get home.'

'Love you too, Bye.'

Unknown to her, although she was out of sight her conversation with David was overheard by Michael. He was not too pleased with what he heard.

'That was an interesting call you made;' he said with an air of sarcasm.

She was annoyed that she had been indiscrete and also that Michael should be commenting on the call. She kept her feelings under control and tried to answer as calmly as possible.

'David is a friend, nothing more!'

'This sounds more than just a friend - Mum!'

'What do you mean by that?' Her voice was raised.

'Well, darling this and darling that!' he replied.

Now she was flustered and felt like she was losing some self control.

'It's nothing like that, and if it was, it's nothing to do with you!'

Michael was quick tempered, a trait he inherited from his father. She knew that and anticipated an angry response.

'It has got something to do with me. It's not right at your age and it's not right for Dad's sake, I mean for the memory of Dad!'

'For goodness sake, your Dad has been dead for four years!'

She stopped. She knew she had gone too far.

'I am so sorry Michael. I didn't mean to say that, I am sorry.'

Michael was angry and distressed. He had been very close to his father, more so than his mother. He still cherished fond memories and could not accept the thought of his mother doing what he now suspected.

'I just do not like this. It's not right what you are doing!'

'Elizabeth was now regretting that her overheard call had caused such harm. She realised that the chance of gently breaking the news of her new found love had gone. It was time to tell all.

'Michael, listen to me;' she pleaded.

'David is first and foremost a friend. He's a widower. His wife died a year ago. We got talking because we had a lot in common. Now we are closer, we support each other, we are companions and I have a deep affection for him!'

Michael interrupted her. 'I don't want to hear anymore Mum. What you are doing is not right. Dad's memory means more than that. I cannot accept another man taking his place!' He looked towards his wife for support. But Margaret did not want to get involved in such a sensitive matter and she was faced with a dilemma. She felt duty bound to support her husband, but she had some sympathy for the way that her mother in law was determined to seek an alternative to the life her son expected of her as a widow.

'Don't you agree with me Margaret?' he asked.

Margaret hesitated. She had to tread very carefully.

'Of course I do;' she replied. 'All of this has come as a complete shock. You are bound to be upset.'

She turned to look at Elizabeth.

'Perhaps if you had let Michael know sooner, he might have been more understanding.'

Elizabeth was quietly content that Margaret had not condemned her in the manner of her son. But Michael was not so happy with his wife's response.

'No way!' he responded. 'It would not matter how you told me. There is no way I would ever think this was the right thing to do!'

Her remaining time with her family was cool and guarded. She obtained some consolation from quality time with her grandson who was innocently unaware of the rift developing between his Grandmother and his Father. Before she left the following morning to return to Southport she spoke to Margaret. Her son had gone to work so they were alone.

'I'm really sorry to have caused all this trouble with Michael. It was not how I intended it to happen.'

Margaret put aside her usual restraint towards her mother in law and replied.

'It is a pity. Michael has always seen his father as his idol. When his Dad died he took it badly and he still feels that way. I just hope he will come round to accept what you are doing.'

Elizabeth embraced Margaret. 'Thank you.' She whispered.

Margaret replied. 'I wish you all the luck in the world.'


Her feeling of despondency finally vanished when she stood on the station platform and saw a smiling David coming towards her. They were glad to be together again. David picked up her luggage and escorted her to his car.

'How was the trip?' he asked.

'It didn't go too well, so I am really glad to be home. I'll tell you all about it later.' she replied.

He drove into the forecourt of the flats and offered to carry her bag to the lift. When they reached the lift she asked,

'Would you like to come up for a minute? I can offer you an instant coffee - without milk of course!'

'Thanks, I would like that, just for a little while. It's getting late:' he replied.

She opened the door to her flat and invited him in. It was dark so she switched on the hall light and invited him into her lounge. This was his first time in the flat and he was impressed with how comfortable and orderly it was. Elizabeth excused herself and went into her kitchen to make the promised coffee. She brought in two mugs of coffee and an unopened box of chocolate biscuits.

'Sorry I don't have anything else to offer.'

'This is fine, seeing you again is enough;' he replied.

Both were keen to hear how each got on with their families and any reactions to hints of their blossoming romance. Elizabeth got her question in first.

'Tell me how you got on with Julie and how about remembering Clare?'

He gave as much detail as he could recall and finally got round to the delicate subject.

'It went well actually. It came as a bit of a shock to Julie at first, but she took it well and seemed to accept that you and I were happy together. James seemed pleased too, probable because it could delay the day I might need to go down there to be near to them,

'But what about you, how did you get on?' he asked.

'It didn't go well at all;' she replied.

''Remember when I phoned you?

David nodded and motioned her to continue.

'Well I didn't realise it at the time, but Michael overheard me talking. He put two and two together and blew his top. He does not approve our relationship. It's because of his memory of his Dad. I can understand that and feel ashamed about the way he heard our call. I don't think he can ever accept that someone else could replace his Dad,'

David could see that she was very upset and was afraid it might end their own relationship. He leaned forward to console her.
'Michael will come round to accept us being together in good time.'
'I don't think so;' she said, knowing how stubborn her son could be.
'I cannot see how it will be possible for me to go down there again!'
It was hard for David to understand how a family relationship could be so damaged by such a simple occurrence. He hesitated before saying.
'Try not to worry, we still have each other.'
She leaned forward to hold his hand and he was reassured that he had not said anything out of place. At that moment they both found a new sense of freedom. They could now be more open about their affair. The anniversary of David's late wife's death was behind them and for better or worse there families were now fully aware of their circumstances.

The following day they celebrated their new found freedom by driving into Liverpool. David parked his car at the waterfront close to the Albert Dock. They walked past the new arena and the modern developments surrounding it. The river Mersey was in full flow at high tide and the river was busy with shipping taking advantage of the tide.

The river was choppy as they stopped to take in the panoramic view before them. They made a brief visit to the Tate Gallery and then the Maritime Museum, both in the dock complex. In the museum they were engrossed by the maritime history of the City. The displays illustrated the city's involvement in the slave trade and the mass emigration of families on their way to find new lives in America and Canada.

They continued their walk past the famous World Heritage site of the three buildings known as the Three Graces. Beyond the ferry terminal they sighted a gigantic cruise liner docked alongside the cruise terminal. They were in time to see passengers coming through the gates intent on exploring the sites of the City. Two young American tourists asked to be directed to the Beatles Exhibition. Elizabeth smiled at the thought that the couple could be descendents of families who embarked from the same spot many generations ago.

They spent the rest of the afternoon sitting by the riverside. This was a place of constant activity. The Mersey Ferry made regular crossings to Birkenhead on the opposite side of the river with passengers coming and going. Occasionally larger ocean going ships would pass on their way up river to the oil terminal or out towards the Irish Sea.

## Chapter Five

## Banishing the Demons

They left Liverpool late in the afternoon in time to join the end of day exodus out of the city. So David took a detour off the main road into Crosby. There they found a quiet pub for a leisurely evening meal before resuming their journey back to Southport. When they arrived he invited Elizabeth back to his place before dropping her off at her flat. They settled down in the lounge with their usual cup of coffee. There was a brief moment of silence before she said;

'You know dear! You never finished telling me about how you coped with Clare's dementia. You need to finish your story!'

'Yes I did promise you;' he replied.

'I told you about the operation on her legs. She was very distressed after that. From then onwards things got worse. For no apparent reason she became very upset in our car. Even short journeys from shopping upset her. When she took these turns it became very difficult for me to drive and try to calm her at the same time. Gradually she lost her confidence and her lack of coordination got to the point where I could not leave her alone in our kitchen. We still managed to do things together and get out but it became more and more difficult. She was never ever violent. In fact she was very placid apart from these panic attacks. She never complained or explained what was going on inside her head so it was so difficult to know what to do to help her.'

He paused to gather his thoughts. 'It was a very slow, slow journey down a dark road with no guiding light!'

'Why did you not get outside help? she asked.

'I tried!' he replied.

'I phoned the Social Services and they sent someone round to carry out an assessment of our needs. But in truth the only assessment they were interested in was our financial status. They could have done that while walking up our drive without coming into the house! The State would support Clare if we were poor or any assets we had were below their limit. If our assets were above that limit which obviously they were, then we were on our own! We were left with a handful of information booklets and lists of care homes and charity contacts. An assessment report came through the post a couple of weeks later, but that was the last I heard from them. Maybe I'm being a bit unfair because there was a care allowance which we got after another assessment. That helped'

Elizabeth remarked. 'I didn't realise that could happen in this day and age. You both worked all your lives, paid your dues and the State deserts you when you need it most.'

'I know!' he replied. 'By this time I was feeling the strain and in need of a break.'

'I had two options, Clare could go into a Care Home or I could bring in care workers to look after her at home. So I looked through the stuff they left to find a care home that took in dementia patients. I checked their fancy web sites and their quality ratings. One place looked promising. I was looking for a place that would take Clare for a week to give me some respite. But it wasn't a case of just making a booking like in a hotel. An appointment was made for somebody to come to make yet another assessment. Two people turned up. The lady was interested in Clare's condition and took lots of notes which I expected. But her male companion was obviously the money man who was there to assess my ability to pay the seven hundred pounds quoted for the week. I think he had a longer stay in mind!'

'I fixed a date and was invited to call in anytime before, to look around the premises. We did that, turning up one afternoon shortly after lunch for an unannounced visit. I rang the door bell and after a few minutes it was opened cautiously by a young girl who looked like one of the care assistants. I said we had been invited to visit the place. We were ushered into the hallway and told to wait while the girl left us to find someone more senior to meet us.'

'The residents must have just finished their lunch. Some were passing us to go into the lounge where I could see it was full of an assortment of armchairs spread around all four walls. Others were aimlessly shuffling about in the corridor. There must have been more than thirty men and women all showing various degrees of dementia. I recognised the similarities to Clare's condition. But to my shame my reactions were different. I felt very depressed at the sight of people who looked abandoned except for the few carers that attended to them.'

'The lady who visited us at home met us in the hall and accompanied us on our visit.'

We went into the lounge where some of the residents were seated. An elderly lady looked at us and asked the carer who we were?'

'This is Clare, she is coming to stay with us!' she replied.

'That wasn't my intention. It sounded too permanent for my liking.'

We continued our tour passing many a poor soul on the way. We finished in the bedroom that had been held for Clare. It was very small, sparsely furnished but clean. Clare never said a word but I knew she would never be happy there and feared if I left here there the chance was that she would never come out.'

'Later that evening I was uneasy. I came to a disturbing conclusion. These poor souls were not there by choice. I felt that most were cast offs of our society where families could not or would not care for their old and sick. I decided I could not abandon her in that way. I felt I would be placing her in God's Waiting Room! The following morning I phoned and cancelled the reservation!'

Elizabeth was confused at what David was saying. She had a different view of care homes but hesitated to question what she had just heard. David sensed her doubts.

'Maybe I was being unfair on the place at the time. It had a good quality rating and the carers obviously had a difficult time dealing with the complicated needs of the residents. Unfortunately this is the modern way that society deals with the elderly and the sick.'

He knew he had said enough about that experience and quickly changed the subject.

'Weeks and months were just a jumble in my mind. I can remember that different problems were affecting her health. The stairs became a problem because she was unsteady. Her appetite was going and her height and weight were noticeably diminishing. She had difficulty with her false teeth and they were eventually abandoned. But worst of all, the incontinence changed to severe constipation. I took her to the doctor and she arranged for the District Nurse to call to do the necessary! She turned up once and grumbled that she could not handle Clare on her own, so I had to help get Clare positioned on the bed. I never saw the nurse again and finished up doing the job myself.'

'I had hoped that some of her physical problems might have been treated in hospital, but that never happened. I felt that dementia patients were not welcome in hospital wards, perhaps for good reasons. 'But you know, tasks like that didn't bother me or Clare. However, it was difficult to get her out of bed and into the bathroom. She would resist like hell by planting her hands against the door or digging her feet into the carpet. This became a daily ritual and a struggle and I never knew why she did it.'

'On the lighter side, I worked out a great way to get her washed in the morning which amused us. The technique was simple but effective. She would sit on the toilet and I placed a plastic basin of soapy water on her lap. Washing her hands and face became a game. Other parts had to be washed and that wasn't quite so simple! But we did manage without the need for outside help.'

'Another option to get some respite for both of us was a Daily Care Centre where she could go for the day and give me an extended break. This had a lot of appeal so I found a place that was run by the Council, but of course it wasn't free to us. At first this was ideal. I would take Clare in the morning and they provided a light breakfast and a full lunch then I collected her in the afternoon. Some of the old people were infirm and not all suffered from dementia, so the atmosphere in the centre was good and she made friends. I appreciated a full days respite but new difficulties appeared at home.'

'We had to be at the centre for nine in the morning in time for her breakfast. Getting Clare ready became a real issue for me. On a good day it took as much as an hour to get her out of bed, washed, and dressed. Most days were bad! Then there was the journey in the car and the panic attacks. She attended the centre for about six months when the manager asked to speak to me. She had noticed Clare's condition. Her anxiety and general health was a concern. The centre had an arrangement with a local hospital to call in a doctor or consultant when they needed advice or help. The manager suggested I might like this to happen to try and assess Clare's condition. I willingly agreed because any professional advice would be welcome.'

'An appointment was made for us to go to the day centre to meet a Consultant Psychiatrist. At the end of the interview he said he would advise Claire's doctor to prescribe a drug that would alleviate her anxiety. What happened next, I will never forget. I gave Clare her first tablet before going to bed. The following morning I woke her up as usual. She smiled at me, said a few words and without any assistance she walked to the bathroom. You can imagine how surprised and delighted I felt. After lunch we got into the car and went for a walk along Southport pier. We stopped at the café at the end of the pier for a cup of tea. Then suddenly I saw that change in her eyes and knew it was time to get her back home quickly. She never recovered that brief moment of near normality.'

'The only way I can explain what happened is, well, you know if you have an electric light bulb that is on its last legs and when you switch it on there is a bright flash before it fails? Well that is how it was for Clare!'

'She never recovered that brief moment. We carried on at the day centre for a short time until one day, early in the afternoon, I received a call from the manager. She asked me to book an emergency appointment at our surgery and come and collect Clare. She was worried about Clare's health and thought she was severely dehydrated. I got an appointment that afternoon. The doctor examined Clare and did not seem so concerned as the day centre. She prescribed a course of liquid energy drinks and advice on a suitable diet to address her weight loss. All this time I kept thinking why is she not being referred to the hospital? Was it dementia that was depriving her of treatment any normal person would expect?'

'Clare never went back to the day centre after that so I was faced with the final option of finding suitable care. We still had moments when she seemed content in our own home so I was determined to keep caring for her. But I knew that the demands were becoming increasingly difficult.. So I looked at bringing in Home Care assistance. I was cautious about this, partly because of criticisms of the service and also because of the cost based on an hourly rate. I contacted a good provider and the usual assessment had to be made so that a suitable carer could be allocated to look after Clare. It was agreed at first to have the carer come in for an hour in the morning to wash and dress Clare and provide her breakfast. The service was to start in two weeks time so that suitable arrangements could be made.'

'Before this could be organised, Clare's condition seriously deteriorated. I called the surgery to get her doctor to come to the house. The doctor was concerned but she did not send her to the hospital. She made a call and at last some positive action took place.'

'The following day, a senior nurse arrived from the hospital. She was in charge of a special unit that provided emergency care in the home. Within a few days they delivered a hospital bed with a special mattress and an invalid chair and, would you believe it! Two large boxes of NHS incontinence pads, all free of charge! This all had to go upstairs to be near the bathroom which meant that Clare was confined there because she could no longer use the stairs. 'Every morning two nurses arrived to wash and dress Clare. They sat her on the chair where she stayed for the rest of the day. This care was only supposed to last for a few days, but the nurses turned up for nearly two weeks until the home carer took over.'

'I knew I was losing Clare and she knew within herself that her time was ebbing away. She was very placid, sitting by the bedroom window, watching the world go by. Only once did she show any feelings. 'I'm going to die!' she cried and all I could do was to try and calm her down.'

'A week after the nursing care finished the senior nurse from the hospital returned to see how we were coping. She went upstairs to see Clare. When she came down she spoke to me.'

'I am afraid Clare is nearing the end of life.'

'I knew she was speaking from long experience and there was no need for me to question her judgement.'

The nurse asked me; 'Has your doctor spoken to you about signing a DNR form? It means do not resuscitate. It can save further suffering for patients like Clare should circumstances require medical staff to take that decision.'

'I understood the implications of what she was saying and agreed that I would sign the form, although I still have mixed feelings about what I did.'

'The carer came in every morning for an hour to wash and dress her and help with her breakfast. This was either porridge or scrambled egg which I brought up from the kitchen. The carer had a good way with Clare and could raise a smile and a few words of conversation. One Friday morning I came into the bedroom just as the carer was writing up her daily report. She looked at me and said.'

'We had a nice chat today, didn't we Clare? She told me you were a good man.'

David recollected. 'I remember Clare looking at me with a faint smile on her face.
That was her last smile!'

'Clare sat in her chair for the rest of that day. I took up her evening meal. When we finished I wheeled the chair into the hall and helped her out of the chair so she could walk the short distance to the bathroom. Suddenly her arms went limp. She took a few steps then her legs buckled under her and she collapsed on the hall landing. I tried to make her comfortable but I could not lift her back into the bedroom. I called 999 and explained the situation. The responder called up an ambulance straight away. She asked if Clare was still breathing. I said she was so the responder insisted that I follow her instructions to give artificial respiration. She kept repeating the ambulance is on its way, keep going. It was a nightmare that still haunts me. I had signed a DNR but there was no way I could say that over the phone. So I kept going although I wanted to stop to comfort her. She died in my arms just as the ambulance arrived. I left Clare to go down stairs and open the door. The crew rushed upstairs to attend to her, but they knew they were too late. They asked me about resuscitation and I handed them the form that authorised them not to proceed.'

David stopped there, he knew he had said more that enough but he felt a sense of relief from his hidden thoughts. He looked at Elizabeth who was visibly upset with tears on her cheeks. He moved closer to her and knelled beside her.

'I'm sorry if all this has upset you. All I can say is thank you for listening. You have helped me so much. I hope these bad memories have now gone.'

# Chapter Six

## A Blossoming Relationship

Any inhibitions they had about declaring their new found love for each other had gone. They were comfortable in each others company and indifferent to any criticism that might come their way. An early opportunity to be open about this happened at a social club meeting. David deliberately sat at the table with Elizabeth amongst her usual group of ladies. They did not need to be obvious about their new friendship. The ladies soon conjured up their own scenarios. This truly was fertile ground to cast the seeds of gossip. The weeks that followed were a new adventure for the couple. Visits to the cinema were no longer secretive. They enjoyed going to the theatre, lunch and dinner occasions and occasional journeys to places of interest by car.

Another opportunity to establish their relationship came about when they received separate invitations from mutual friends to attend their wedding anniversary. The reception was to be held in the hotel on the Promenade. Although they might have been expected to turn up on their own, they decided to go together as a couple, not knowing whether their new relationship would be known or appreciated by the guests.

David collected Elizabeth from her flat. He opened his car door and helped her to fasten the safety belt. He was taken aback by how attractive she looked. Her hair had been styled and she looked very attractive in her evening attire. He got into the car and noted the air was filled by the aroma of her perfume. It had not occurred to him that she would go to such lengths to be so attractive. He was reasonably smartly dressed in slacks and sports jacket and thought it would be in order not to wear a tie.

He was aware that he had not really matched his attire to that of Elizabeth and hoped she was not upset.
'You're looking really lovely tonight;' he said.
'Thank you dear, your not so bad yourself;' she replied.
'I'm not really dressed to complement your outfit. I hope you are not too disappointed.'
'Don't be silly. Men are not expected to go to the extremes of us girls!'
He drove into the hotel's underground car park and they made their way up into the hotel foyer. A notice directed them to the reception room where there hosts Mary and Brian were greeting arriving guests. Elizabeth was carrying a small gift bag which she handed to Mary.
'Congratulations, this is from both of us to both of you.'
They had agreed beforehand that it was time to fly their flag and a joint gift was a good opportunity to do that.
'Oh how interesting, thank you both very much.' replied Mary.

Her husband was a little puzzled at this exchange, as Mary directed them into the room with a knowing smile.

'Find a table and get yourself a drink, the bar is open.'

She held Elizabeth's arm. 'We'll have a little chat later.'

They looked around the room to see where it was best to sit. They could see the room was full of a number of round tables each seating eight. The tables were laid out for an expensive celebration and were decorated tastefully with a central flower display. Most of the tables were occupied and the occupants were fully engaged in conversation. One table had spare seats where two of Elizabeth's friends and their husbands were seated. Elizabeth pointed this out to David and he dutifully followed. As they made there way towards the table he was conscious of a number of heads turned towards them and could only assume that they were the subject of some interest. They seated themselves and David asked Elizabeth if she would like a drink from the bar. She asked for a glass of red wine and he restricted himself to a soft drink, regretting that they had not come by taxi instead of his car.

Celebration proceedings went well and by the time formalities were over their table companions had consumed the best part of two bottles of wine. Tongues were freed of inhibition and inevitably the conversation turned to their relationship. One of the ladies turned to Elizabeth and said:

'You and David look great together are you an item?'

'An item, what does that mean?' she thought.

'We are very good friends, that's all!' Elizabeth replied.

'Oh, come on it must be more than that. How long have you been together?' the lady asked.

David did not like the way the conversation might go so he interrupted them.

'We have known each other for a long time as you know, so it's not what you might be thinking. We are good friends because we have common interests that keep us together.'

He realised that his intervention was slightly ambiguous but it was enough to change the subject. It was fine to be seen together but he had no wish to be quizzed on the more intimate parts of their relationship. The formal part of the reception ended and some of the guests were retreating to the hotel bar. David motioned Elizabeth to the outside veranda where they were joined by their hosts who were pleased to share this quiet spot. They sat together enjoying the view over the lake and beyond to the Estuary. The sun was low over the horizon, illuminating the pier in a brilliant orange glow.

Mary opened the conversation 'It was a real surprise to see you both. How long have you been together?'

David replied. 'As you know, Clare passed away some time ago and Elizabeth was a great help to me. It's hard to explain how difficult life becomes when you lose someone you spent most of your life with.'

Elizabeth added. 'We were both in a similar situation and somehow we found that we supported each other. But ours is a partnership, don't expect us to be announcing an engagement or anything like that.'

They all laughed at the forcefulness of her statement before Brian added.

'I should hope not! Make the most of what you have without all the hassle of marriage and the inevitable trouble with the family. You know what I mean, inheritance and all that!'

They successfully weathered the rest of the evening and were happy that they had broken the ice without falling into the hole. At the end of the evening they said there farewells to their hosts, with a parting quip from Mary.

'Be good!'

'We will!' replied David.

Elizabeth had consumed more wine than she was used to, so she was slightly unsteady on her feet and more talkative than usual. The cool evening air was refreshing. She looked at David and said.

'I don't want to go home straight away. Can we go for a drive somewhere?'

David was perfectly sober so her request was more than welcome.

'That's a good idea. I know the perfect place,'

He drove out of the hotel car park on to the Promenade past the Marine Lake then turned into the Esplanade. He drove into the deserted car park overlooking the sea. The night sky was dark, except for the afterglow of the sun reflected from high clouds onto the waves as they splashed onto the beach,

'Will this do?' he asked.

'Perfect.' she replied 'I haven't done anything like this for years. Long before I got married.'

They sat quietly for a time, taking in the stillness of the night and alone with their own thought until David broke the silence.

'I thought Brian came over as being against marriage. I don't think Mary was too impressed.'

'Have you ever thought of getting married again? Elizabeth asked.

'Not until recently, is this a proposal? he joked.

'Don't be silly it's a hypothetical question.'

'That's a shame!' he replied before giving her question some thought.

'Marriage at our age is too complicated. When you are young it's much easier because it's a beginning. It's the expected thing to do and your responsibilities are less. At our age it's different. For a start it's not normal, we are expected to stay loyal to our past. Then there is our legacy, getting married complicates that because of the expectations of our children when we pass on. Then there is the physical side and I am not talking about sex. How do two people who are set in their ways, with health problems and personal habits cope with being married?'

He continued; 'Then of course there is the question of sex - but don't mention it to the kids!'

They laughed together at this last remark and both thought. 'What about sex?' without knowing the answer.

The sun had long since disappeared over the horizon when suddenly the darkness was broken by the headlights of an approaching car. The car stopped and David immediately recognised it as a police car. The driver was looking at them and they were clearly conspicuous as the only car in the otherwise empty car park. David thought about giving an acknowledging signal then hesitated thinking the policeman might misinterpret his signal as a rude gesture. So they both sat upright not knowing what would happen next. The policemen in the car were obviously checking them out.

'There clocking my registration number.' he said.

'I hope your tax is up to date!' she replied.

'It was renewed last week. I hope the DVLA records are up to date!'

Elizabeth burst into an uncontrollable fit of laughter. 'This is so embarrassing just imagine. What if it got into our local newspaper?' They relaxed as the police car slowly went on its way. Then she had another thought. 'Are we supposed to have a parking ticket here at this time?'

'I don't know!' he replied. 'If they come back again things could get tricky so it's time I took you back home.' They departed the scene with Elizabeth in an uncontrollable state of giggles!

Their relationship was blossoming into a good feeling of happiness that neither had experienced in a long time. There was no tension between them but external pressures were always present. David's relationship with Julie was in good shape. He arranged a meeting between his daughter and Elizabeth when she came up to stay for a few days. They got on well together, which pleased him. Before leaving for home Julie remarked.

'Dad, Elizabeth is really nice. I like her, she reminds me of Mum!' Her reply raised a doubt in his mind because he had not formed that opinion. He wondered if this was why he was so attracted to Elizabeth. If it was a subconscious thing then it was unfair on Elizabeth. He quickly dismissed the idea but was pleased that Julie was fond of Elizabeth.

Relations between Elizabeth and her son Michael were still strained and she had no idea how to bring him round to accept David as her partner. She missed seeing her grandson Stephen and was hurt when she missed his birthday. Normally she would have been expected to visit them but no invitation was received. She made occasional telephone calls which were usually answered by her daughter in law. When she did speak to Michael, he was curt and David was never mentioned. She knew that one day some form of reconciliation would need to take place, but she had no idea how.

# Chapter Seven

## A Cunning Plan

Nearly a year has passed since David wrote his fateful letter. Their friendship remained strong. It was early springtime and the day was warm and sunny so they decided to go for a walk in Hesketh Park. They stopped by the lake to admire the fountain and watch the swans being fed nearby. Suddenly Elizabeth plucked a question out of her head.

'David, when did you last have a holiday?' she asked.

'A long time ago before Clare got ill and we had to cancel two holidays after that.'

'You should take a holiday now. No reason for not going somewhere nice for a week's break;' she replied.

'It's not so easy when you are on your own. Most holidays are geared up for couples and you have to pay steep supplements if you want a single room. When you get there the chances are that you will be miserable in a strange place1'

'You are being silly, you are just making excuses.' she replied.

'No I'm not.' he answered then out of the blue he asked.

'Why don't we go together? That would be fun.'

She was surprised but not adverse to the suggestion.

'It would still be expensive.' she replied.

'Why?'

'Single rooms and all that!'

'We could share!' he said in a persuasive tone of voice.

Now she really was shocked.

'That would not work. It would be too embarrassing. It could be the end of a perfect friendship!' She looked at him and waited for a response.

'It could be the beginning!' he replied.

'I cannot see how that would work. How do you make the booking? In separate names or fake identities?'

He replied: 'That's old fashioned. Unmarried couples or partners have been doing it for years!'

'Oh, I would be too embarrassed.' She whispered with a slight shiver of her shoulders.

'Okay!' he paused. 'Let's have a trial. Come and stay at my place for a night. You could sleep in the spare bedroom. You can even lock the door if you think I might be naughty.'

It sounded like a crazy suggestion, but somehow it interested her. She struggled to find convincing objections to the idea. Then another thought came to mind.

'I couldn't leave the car at your place overnight. That would really get your neighbours tongues waging, and what about my neighbour? Grace and I look out for each other. She would know and be worried if I was out of my flat overnight.'

David smiled and said, 'Don't worry, I have a *cunning plan*!'
She was amused by his Blackadder impersonation.

'So what is this cunning plan?'

He set out his plan. She did not need to use her car as he would collect her in his car. As far as Grace was concerned, she should say she was staying overnight with a friend. She was to pack an overnight bag and phone him when she was ready and he would pick her up at the nearby bus stop.

It all sounded too simple for her; 'How do you get me into the house without the neighbours knowing? Do I need to hide myself in the back seat?

'No, no, I would not ask you to do that. Anyway nobody is going to notice.'

'So how do I get out of the car and through the front door without being noticed?'

He was now about to reveal more of his plan.

'You stay in the car for a couple of minutes while I drive it into the garage. I get out and close the garage doors, go into the house on my own. I go into the back garden and open the side door to the garage. You get out and - *hay presto*! You are in.'

Elizabeth smiled. 'You didn't think that up here and now. You naughty man, how long have you been hatching this up?'

He was not prepared to answer the question so he quickly replied.

'All we need to do is pick a day or should I say a night?'

She could find no more objections to the plan and was inwardly excited at the thought of what was to come. They agreed the following Saturday into Sunday would be best, leaving only a few days for them to wait.

David spent more time than usual dusting and generally cleaning his house. He promised Elizabeth that she could sleep in the spare bedroom so it received special attention and was liberally sprayed with air freshener. He retrieved a new set of bed linen from a cupboard to make her as comfortable as possible. He also took the precaution of changing the bed linen in his own room.

As promised, she phoned him just after six o clock in the evening. He picked up the receiver.

'How are you getting on?' he asked.

'I'm packed and ready to go.'

'Good! I should be at your bus stop in five minutes. If you leave now we should meet about the same time.' He arrived just as she was crossing the main road.

'Do I go in the front or the back?' she asked.

He replied. 'Don't be silly, sit beside me.'

He then asked, 'Have you had any supper yet?'

She had not, so he made a suggestion.

'How would you like some fish and chips from the Chippy?'

'Sounds good!' she replied, so he stopped off at the local shop, leaving her sitting in the car. Five minutes later he emerged carrying the takeaway evening meal.

The *cunning plan* went according to plan and Elizabeth, unseen by inquisitive eyes, was seated at the kitchen table enjoying her evening meal. The rest of the evening passed quietly as they chatted in the lounge. The bottle of wine opened earlier was empty and the television was humming away in the background, unseen and unheard.

They sat there for a long time, it was getting late and thoughts turned to bedtime. Earlier in the evening he took Elizabeth's bag up to the bedroom. He closed the curtains and switched on the bedside lamp. Now he escorted her up the stairs opened the door and ushered her into the room. The room was warm and inviting and she could see he had gone to some trouble to make it so.

'I hope everything is to your liking. Towels are there for you so have a shower or bath whenever it suits you. You know where the bathroom is. I hope you sleep well and I'll see you in the morning.'

This was a new experience for both. An experience they had eagerly anticipated, but for the moment they were lost for words.
'The room is lovely David. Thank you, see you in the morning!'

They embraced each other for a moment and he kissed her cheek. He closed the door and made for his own bedroom. Elizabeth sat on the bed. She noticed the key in the door, just as he promised, but she had no thoughts of locking the door. She had learned to trust David and knew he would not take an unfair advantage of her being alone with him in his home. She stood up and turned the duvet cover over to test the softness of the bed. The bed sheet and pillow cases were obviously new, and she smiled, noting the original crease marks from the packaging.

'He might have run an iron over them!' but it was just a passing thought.

The bedroom was much cosier than she remembered and she detected the faint trace of air freshener. So, all in all, she was happy to be here. However she did regret the fish and chip supper. It seemed a good idea at the time, but it was not part of her usual diet and it was making its presence felt. She unpacked her overnight bag and searched for a strip of indigestion tablets in her toilet bag. She also took out a packet of paracetamol tablets because she felt the start of another headache.

These headaches were a worry. She tended not to make too much of a fuss when the headaches appeared and she only occasionally mention her problem to David. The last time she visited the doctor he sent her to the medical centre for a blood test. It took time to make an appointment then she had to wait for the results before going back to the surgery. So she forgot to make another appointment to get the results. When she did remember she thought if there was anything serious in the tests the surgery would have contacted her. She took her medication, slid between the pristine bedclothes and settled down for a peaceful nights sleep.

When David closed his bedroom door he was pleased that the evening had gone so well. He knew now that he would be comfortable with her sharing his home. They still had to be sure it would be the same if they shared the same room, but that was for another day. He got into bed, laid back looking at the ceiling. Then an uneasy feeling worried him. He began to think of his late wife. He thought if Clare was looking down on him what would she think of another woman taking her place in their home? He fell asleep with one thought in his mind. 'Am I being unfair to Clare or to her memory?' For the rest of the night his sleep was disturbed and not what he had hoped for.

He wakened early next morning. There was no sound coming from Elizabeth's room so he took the opportunity of having an early shower. He dressed quickly and headed downstairs. Her door was closed and he assumed she was still asleep. A light breakfast followed and it was now approaching nine o' clock. He decided to take up a cup of tea, mainly to ensure that all was well. He knocked the door quietly and waited for a response.

'Come in David, I'm decent!' she replied.

He partly opened the door and cautiously looked around it. She was still in bed, slightly propped up on her pillows. He noticed how her hair was covered and the straps of her night dress exposed her bare shoulders. She had no make up on and her complexion was paler than he was used to, but he was captivated with the plainness of her beauty. She apologised for still being in bed. Remarking she was taking advantage of not having to go to church this morning.

'I thought you might like a cup of tea;' he said, trying to avoid staring at her as she raised herself to accept the cup.

'Thank you dear. I don't get this service in the flat.'

'I've had my breakfast, but you come down whenever you like;' he added.

'I will, but I think a shower is calling!'

'Take your time;' he replied.

He returned to the kitchen, switched on his radio to catch up with the morning news. The water from her shower was flowing into the garden drain and he mused. 'I've got a naked lady upstairs in my bathroom!' Twenty minutes later she came down stairs, knocked on the kitchen door and walked in. He stared. She was wearing one of his cotton bathrobes and her hair was covered by a wrap around towel.

'I thought it best to come down before getting dressed in case you wanted to get breakfast over with. I can take an age to get ready for the day ahead!' she explained.

'No problem!' he replied.

She added. 'Since this is supposed to be a dummy run, you might as well see me without my armour plating.'

'Elizabeth, you look lovely!' was all that he could say.

He invited her to take a seat at the table.

'What would you like for your breakfast?

'A cup of your lovely tea and a slice of toast will do nicely.' she replied.

He poured out two cups of tea and sat next to her. They chatted quite naturally about day to day things and David thought,

'How great it would be if this was normal for both of them.'

She finished her breakfast and excused herself to go back to the bedroom to do what all ladies do. David waited patiently for her to reappear. 'She's right!' he thought.

'She does take an age to get ready.'

Eventually she did reappear, looking more elegant than ever. Before he could get a word in she asked a very pressing question.

'Now what cunning plan have you got to get me out of here and back to my flat?'

He scratched the top of his head in a comical way and replied.

'Now look at the mess I've got you into!' They both laughed like delinquent children in expectation of being found out.

# Chapter Eight

## A Cottage in the Highlands

There first night together was a success. Elizabeth was comfortable and happy at the way he treated her with respect and the lack of any awkwardness in their new found relationship. When ever the opportunity arose, she would stay overnight. There was no impulsive driving force to have them share a bed. This relationship became the norm with the comfort of being together overcoming any latent sexual drive to compel them to take the next step. Both were conscious that if they did go on holiday together circumstances might dictate otherwise. For the moment they were well accustomed to each others ways and were experienced enough to know that sharing a bed would not be a serious problem.

However, both were subconsciously cautious. David still had the inhibition he felt on the first night of disrespect for his late wife. Elizabeth was cautious because she could not predict the consequence of intimacy. She could not know what he would expect and would she be able to respond and meet these expectations.

They had not forgotten the original purpose of their liaisons was to go on a shared holiday as partners. David raised the subject again. He produced holiday brochures and further information he downloaded from the internet. He had two objectives for this holiday that he offered to Elizabeth.

'I've been doing a bit of research into holiday location's that appeal to me, but you need to tell me what you think.'

She looked at the bundle of brochures on the table.

'You have been busy! So let's see what you have there;' she remarked.

David replied; 'First of all I would love to go back to Scotland and tour in our car. Secondly I would love to find a holiday cottage just for the two of us!'

Elizabeth seemed delighted with his ideas.

'I love your suggestion. It has all we need for a perfect holiday, away from everything and everybody!'

He was pleased with her positive response and selected one brochure from the bundle. The front cover had a heading; *Holiday Cottages in Scotland*. He turned to an earmarked page and handed it to Elizabeth.

'What do you think of this place?' he asked.

She took the brochure and read out the details.

'Original cottage circa 1730 … fully modernised … extended to sleep six … modern kitchen … five miles from Nairn … one and a half acres of land!'

'Wow!' she exclaimed. 'Look at these pictures. It's just perfect!'

'Let's do it', she exclaimed.

Next day he phoned the agent and was told that the cottage was fully booked for the summer season. He left his contact number in the hope that there might be a suitable cancellation. Two days later the agent came back to him. They had a late cancellation. The cottage was vacant for one week in three weeks time. The agent agreed to hold the reservation for a day to give him time to contact Elizabeth.

'Guess what? Remember the cottage was fully booked? Well the agent has just phoned to offer us a cancellation.'

'That's great but when is it for?'

'Three weeks from tomorrow!' he replied.

There was a silence as she pondered on the suitability or otherwise of this late call. A quick check on her wall calendar satisfied her that any engagements there could be cancelled or delayed.

'David! Go ahead and confirm the booking. This chance is too good to miss. How about you? It doesn't give us much time!'

'It's fine with me. I will confirm the booking and come round to your place to have a chat.'

The day arrived. It was going to be a long drive, so they planned to leave early in the morning. David picked up Elizabeth's luggage the night before so she was ready and waiting for him at the entrance to the flats. It was early morning so they made good progress before joining the M6 motorway heading for Carlisle where they joined the M74 that would take them all the way to Scotland. They crossed the border and immediately they were attracted to the road sign directing them to Gretna Green. It was time for a short break so David pulled into the busy car park. This was a popular place for travellers with its romantic association with runaway lovers.

After refreshments they had time to look at the shops and their displays of tourist gifts. Elizabeth bought some local products that would be useful during their time at the cottage. Then they wandered into the old blacksmiths shop where the marriages once were performed. David asked an attendant to take a picture of them posing beside the anvil. He checked the result on his mobile phone and handed it to Elizabeth.

'Look at that! It looks like we just got married;' he exclaimed.

'Give me Michael's email address and I'll send him a copy.'

'You'll do nothing of the kind, he would have a fit;' she replied.

'Anyway, he doesn't know we are on holiday together. I didn't have the courage to let him know!'

David was surprised at her remark. He had no problems telling his daughter and felt pity for her not being able to speak to her son about such a happy occasion. He said nothing, looked at his watch and suggested it was time to get on their way. They continued their journey on the motorway until they approached Glasgow where they successfully negotiated a series of junctions before joining the M9 and signposts directing them to Perth. By this time Elizabeth was worried that they were heading in the wrong direction.

'Perth is on the east coast, I thought we were supposed to be going north to Inverness?' she asked.

He assured her they were on the correct route because it was quicker than the picturesque western route which he was keeping for their return journey home.

They bypassed Stirling with its view of the distant castle perched high up on a hill. Then they reached Perth and headed towards Pitlochry through the Forest of Athol and the magnificent Grampian Mountains. Now they were heading towards Inverness but the last part of the journey diverted them towards Nairn. Following the instructions proved more difficult than expected but eventually he found the narrow road that led to their destination.

First impressions were mixed. The cottage certainly was isolated and there was no sign of human habitation to be seen. Elizabeth stepped out of the car and opened the gates to allow David to drive into the cottage grounds. They took a moment to look around. The cottage was larger than expected because the modern extension matched the original building. They admired the grounds which looked well maintained. There was nobody there to meet them. The keys to the cottage were kept in a box beside the door. David had the code number to open the box and they both entered the cottage. A long passageway leading to the modern part of the cottage opened up to a fully equipped kitchen. Beyond was a comfortable lounge with the promised log fire and enough logs to last the duration of their stay. A conservatory extended beyond the lounge and in the early evening light was bright and comfortable. To the left a door opened into the original part of the cottage. They checked out the bathroom and two bedrooms, both with the original stonework tastefully painted in white emulsion. The beds were freshly made up with crisp white linen.

'Which room do you prefer?' asked David.

'I don't mind, they are both lovely;' she replied.

He gallantly offered her the end room because it was bigger and had more natural light.

'That's fine, thank you;' she replied.

They unloaded their luggage from the car, placed suitcases into the respective bedrooms and filled the fridge with the supplies they brought to keep them going until they could stock up locally. They had stopped for a meal on the journey so they were content to settle down in the lounge with a light snack. It was too late to light the log fire but the room was still warm and they felt comfortable in their new surroundings. They chatted awhile then Elizabeth looking at the painted stonework remarked.

'You know, these stones must have witnessed many things. Do you think the stonework in the bedrooms were part of the original cottage?'

'I don't think so;' he replied. 'If the building goes back to the 18th century it would be a lot different from now.'

She acknowledged his words but felt a slight shiver as her imagination took hold.

It was now late evening and dark outside and they had not been able to explore the grounds when they arrived. Elizabeth was busy in the kitchen as David opened the front door to take in the evening air. He called her.

'Elizabeth come and see this!'

She joined him and held his hand. It was dark, a darkness that both had rarely experienced. The sky was clear, and provided a backdrop for more and brighter stars than they had ever witnessed.

'It's breathtaking!' she said.

But inwardly she was feeling uneasy. Her earlier thoughts about the cottage stonework and now this feeling of complete isolation added to her concerns. She linked her arm with David and said:

'This might sound daft, but I think this is a bit scary. I know it's childish. I don't know how I am going to sleep in that bedroom tonight.'

She looked at him, expecting him to dismiss her concern with a joke.

'I know what you mean. We haven't had time to get used to the place. How would it be if we both slept in the one room tonight?'

'That would be lovely, the end of a perfect day,' she replied.

They returned to the security of the cottage, locking the outside door behind them. Elizabeth retired to her bedroom. But it was unlit and she could not find the light switch. As she fumbled around the wall she felt the roughness of the stones and she felt ill at ease. It was only a matter of seconds before she found the light switch but that was enough to set her heart racing.

After securing all the rooms David returned to his bedroom, unpacked his bag and got ready for bed. He quietly knocked on Elizabeth's bedroom door and was invited to enter. She was sitting in front of a dressing table applying the final touches of face cream. There was an electric atmosphere of anticipation. A new experience awaited them. So they both prepared for bed. She folded back the duvet cover and gestured a silent invitation for him to go to bed.

'Which side of the bed do you prefer? he asked.

'I forget!' she exclaimed with an embarrassing laugh.

They both slipped off their dressing gowns and settled a cautious distance from each other. He switched off the bedside lamp and the room was completely black. No distracting light to be seen. They were both very tired after their long journey and sleep took over without any delay.

David was first to awake. He looked towards Elizabeth who was still soundly asleep. He was amused at the slightest sound of snoring. She looked lovely. It was strange that he always thought this at a time when she would have been most concerned about her appearance. He resisted the temptation to lean over and wake her with a kiss. So, he slipped out of bed and made his way to the bathroom and a morning shower. He was out of the shower and drying himself when there was a knock on the door. It was Elizabeth.

'David are you decent? I need to get to the toilet please!'
He wrapped the towel around his middle and opened the door to see her standing in her nightgown.

'Sorry dear sorry!' He said and moved out to make way for her immediate needs. This was an early encounter of the day to day consequences of living together.

Later in the morning they were sitting in the kitchen having breakfast when they heard a noise coming from the front of the cottage. It sounded like a lawn mower and it surprised them after the total silence of the night before. They both went to the window and saw an elderly man in working clothes cutting the grass.

They were about to leave in the car to find there bearings and top up essential supplies, but delayed their journey to go and speak to the gardener.

'Hello! You've got a big job there;' said David.
'Aye a' have;' he replied. 'Are you the new folks?'
'Yes we are here for the week.' replied Elizabeth.

He stopped the mower and was obviously ready to pass the time of day with strangers. Elizabeth opened the conversation.

'This is a lovely place. Are you the owner?'

'No, I do the garden for the couple who own the cottage. This is a good going place for them so the grounds need to be looked after.'

Elizabeth then asked, 'Is the cottage really as old as they say?'

'There has always been a cottage on this site but it has changed many times over the years. It belonged to the lairds up until recently. So there have been lots of tenants, mainly working for a laird. They say the first tenants were a young family with a couple of bairns. The man was caught up in the Jacobean Rebellion and was killed at the Battle of Culloden, just a few miles from here. They were tough on the folks after the battle and the wife and bairns were evicted from the cottage. We know she was transported to Canada because a couple of years ago the owners met an American family who came here because they could trace there ancestry back to one of the bairns that lived here.'

The gardener was enjoying the opportunity to speak to such an attentive audience, so he continued his history lesson.

'This building has seen a lot in its time. It was empty for a long time Then one of the laird's decided to build a small sawmill down there at the bottom of the grounds. The mill shut down over a hundred years ago but if you go down you can see the pit where the water wheel used to be. It was turned by water from the burn.'

'It seems an unusual place for a saw mill!' said David.

'No, it was a good place. The laird owned a lot of forest land and wood was in big demand then. It was built towards the end of the nineteenth century and the cottage was given to the family of the foreman. He and two other lads ran the mill. That was up until the start of the First World War. The laird was an officer in the Gordon Highlanders. So it was no surprise that the three lads signed up and joined the Highlanders to follow their boss. The mill was closed down and the lads went off to Belgium in 1915.'

'The laird and Jammie Ross, the foreman were killed that year. One of the other lads was badly injured and nobody knows what happened to the other lad. The saw mill never opened again and Jammie's wife and his family had to makes way for new tenants who worked for the new laird. The mill was left to decay as you can see now.'

The gardener's tales reinforced Elizabeth's fear for the stones and the tragedies they held. But she cheered up with the thought that she and David were here for only a week and her fears had resulted in unanticipated benefits.

Their first days were enjoyable getting to know the countryside and visiting nearby tourist attractions. On their second day they set off with the intention of visiting the city of Inverness. With only a few miles remaining before reaching their destination they noticed a sign directing them to the Culloden battlefield. Elizabeth excitingly recalled the story told by the gardener. So, they turned off the main road. They arrived at a surprisingly large and busy car park, situated in front of an impressive Heritage Centre. The building housed the usual restaurant and retail outlets. But what impressed them most was the historic information about the battle and its aftermath.

Elizabeth followed this step by step, noting all the significant aspects of this great historic event. Gradually she began to develop an affinity for the families who lived in the cottage and their tragic experiences. She now understood why many of the visitors were from America and Canada, probably retracing the history of their own ancestors. They visited the field where the battle took place. It was eerily silent. For Elizabeth, the cottage, its history and her fascination for its stones took on a more significant meaning.

They arrived back at the cottage in the late afternoon, and decided to explore the grounds and the remains of the saw mill. Something else caught David's attention beyond and behind the cottage. There was another ruined building there with the outline of a small church. They found a gate next to the cottage that led into the graveyard. Some of the stones went back to the eighteenth century and many had the same family name. The atmosphere became rather eerie as the late afternoon sun cast long shadows over the graveyard. This was not good news for

Elizabeth. She was feeling more nervous about the coming night. There was no doubt in her mind about the need to share her bed this night.

While Elizabeth prepared their evening meal, David loaded up the fire with the logs provided by the owners. The log fire was blazing away in time for their meal, to be taken informally in the lounge. He switched the television on, but switched it off again because of the poor quality of the signal. So they sat back in the comfortable arm chairs, talked and enjoyed a glass of local liqueur purchased by David during the day's excursion. They agreed it was time for bed and there was no need to confirm earlier arrangements still applied. Elizabeth went to her bedroom to prepare for bed, leaving David to rake the burnt embers in the fire and to make the cottage secure for the night. He cleaned the empty liqueur glasses and left them to dry on the draining board in the kitchen. He then went into his own bedroom to undress and put on his pyjamas before quietly knocking on her bedroom door. The room was dimly lit by the bedside lamps and he was conscious of that faint aroma from her perfume.

She was sitting up in bed as he entered and she closed the book she was reading.

'Don't stop reading because I'm here!' he said.

'It's not that interesting,' she replied, leaning over to turn the bed covers on his side. He slid between the sheets without saying a word. He turned towards her and put his arms around her waist and kissed her, whispering good night. The bedside light was switched off. He turned again to face her, put his arm around her waist and gently pulled her towards him. She turned to face him and stroked his cheek. They kissed gently, exploring the new found contact between them.

# Chapter Nine

## An Unwelcomed Call

Their holiday was now coming to an end. It was the last evening in the cottage and they had finished their evening meal and were about to make preparations for an early start in the morning. A familiar ringtone from Elizabeth's mobile phone sounded from the bedroom. By the time she retrieved it the caller had hung up but she recognised the number. She returned to the kitchen where David was working. She looked concerned.

'The call's from Michael!' she said. 'I hope he hasn't been trying to call me before because this,' pointing to the phone, 'has been in the bedroom all week.' She redialled Michael's number.

'Hello Michael sorry I missed your call.'

She paused to listen to his reply and David looked on with some apprehension.

'Sorry dear, I should have let you know I would be away.' ….

'Yes, I'm in Scotland for the week.'….

'No, it's not a coach trip.'….

'I'm staying in a lovely cottage … David ….just the two of us!'….

'Calm down Michael!' ….

'Michael, please don't speak like that!'....

David could only guess Michael's reaction, but he could see that she was becoming agitated by whatever her son was saying.

'Don't be such a hypocrite!'....

She was very angry now.

'You and Margaret lived together for three years before you got married was that an affair?'....

'Michael! Your father is dead!'....

'When you visited us you would insist in sharing your bedroom. Your father wasn't very happy about that, but he kept it to himself.'....

'Michael! We are not having a bloody affair!'....

She was near to tears

David was angry at the tone of the one sided conversation. Impulsively he relieved Elizabeth of her phone. He put the phone to his ear and could hear her son's high pitched angry voice. David interrupting him.

'Michael, please stop and listen. It's David here.'....

'I don't particularly want to speak to you either, but calm down you are upsetting your mother!'....

'We are not having a bloody affair as you call it.'....

'Listen! You do not know the meaning of the word. If we are having an affair then it's not our first affair. That affair was a long and happy marriage for both of us. Believe me, this is our last affair and it will last as long as fate permits!'

The conversation finished abruptly David held out her phone and looked at Elizabeth.

'He has hung up on me!'

He saw that she was very upset. She looked agitated, her face was flushed and her hands were shaking. He was concerned because she looked physically unwell. He asked how she was feeling but she only shook her head without uttering a word. Now, he regretted speaking to Michael the way he did, but it was the only way he was able to defend her from further distress.

Elizabeth did not want to respond to David. She was confused and angry and she felt unwell. She was conscious that her heart rate was too high and she was fearful of her recurring illness because her temples were throbbing. Slowly she began to rationalise her feelings. Her anger was directed towards everyone including herself. She was angry with Michael for what he said. She was distressed and angry at the way she responded to her son and the words she had used. She was also angry with David. Not so much for taking the phone from her hand, but more for seeming to agree with Michael that they were having an affair. To her an affair meant an illicit sexual thing. She could not accept that her marriage and her present relationship to David could be described in these terms.

For the moment she did not wish to discuss these matters with David. Uncertainty about their future was lingering at the back of her mind. She was too confused and unwell to confront him with these negative thoughts. Instinctively she looked at him and said.

'David tomorrow is going to be a long day for you. For both our sakes I think we shouldn't sleep together tonight.'

David was shocked by her suggestion. He didn't react openly to it or try to change her mind. Recognising her emotional state of mind, he reluctantly agreed with her request.

They left the lounge to retire to the separate bedrooms to finish packing for the journey home. Elizabeth stayed in her room so he knocked the door and entered to wish her good night. She returned his greeting but he felt a coolness that was new to him. He could only hope she would feel better in the morning and pray that no permanent damage had been done. He returned to his bedroom and smiled at the sight of his bed that was as it was when he arrived. It was unused for the past six nights.

While preparing for bed, Elizabeth suddenly became conscious of the stone walls. Her superstition took hold and she thought tonight would be one more drama for the walls to store in their cold memory. She took her medication and decided to leave the bedside lamps on all night. There was nobody to cuddle up to if her fears took hold.

Neither of them had a good sleep that night. David was grumpy at the thought of the long drive home. Elizabeth had calmed down a little and was trying to come to terms with yesterday's drama, but there was one thing she needed to clarify from David.

By the time they finished breakfast and made final arrangements to vacate the cottage, normality was returning and she apologised for her stupidity in denying him one last night together. She was now calm enough to ask her question.

'David, yesterday when Michael was on the phone he accused both of us of having an affair. When you took the phone to speak to him you seemed to agree that we were having an affair.'

She paused to judge his reaction. Then she continued. 'I was shocked because I always thought affairs were illicit sexual liaisons, usually at the expense of others. That's not what we are having surely?'

David now understood her concern and realised why she was so cool towards him after the call.

'Elizabeth, if you can remember, I said to Michael that he didn't understand the meaning of the word. If you check it in a modern dictionary you will find that it has two meanings. One meaning is your view that it means an illicit sexual relationship. The other meaning is the one that defines us. It means a relationship of people in love with each other.' She was pleasantly surprised and pleased at his explanation.

'What made you find this out?' she asked.

'It's not the first time I've been accused of us having an affair so I checked it out in a dictionary and liked what I saw!'

He looked at her with a knowing grin on his face and winked his eye.

Equilibrium in their relationship was now restored. They packed the luggage into the car, did a final check that the cottage was as they found it. He returned the key to its box beside the door. Elizabeth closed the gates behind her and they were off to find the scenic route back home. David drove towards Inverness where they picked up the A82 which would take them all the way to Glasgow. The route took them to the top of Loch Ness and the start of a sixty mile journey through the Great Glen.

They stopped briefly to admire the ruins of Urquart Castle built on a promontory of the loch. Elizabeth was entranced by the ruins and her new found interest in the stories they could tell. 'Do you know this castle goes back to the thirteenth century and it was an important part of Scotland's history for hundreds of years;' she said.

Their journey took them down the full length of the lock with its dark and forbidding water until they reached Invergary. This led on to Loch Lochy. At the end of this loch the route turned east towards Fort William where the magnificent Ben Nevis came into view with it summit covered in cloud.

Driving further to the east they came to Glen Coe where they stopped to admire the scenery. Their journey continued through Rannoch Moor towards Crianlarch where they joined the third and most famous Loch Lomand. The road followed the loch for its full length until eventually they reached the west of Glasgow and crossed the River Clyde at Old Kilpatrick to join up with the M8 motorway and then on to the M74 and onwards south towards home.

The never ending winding road from Inverness to Glasgow took much longer to travel and it was late in the evening when they arrived at David's home. They both agreed that it would be best for Elizabeth to stay the night there and save her the trouble of settling into her empty flat at that late hour. He suggested they leave the luggage in the car for the night and she waited by the door until he opened up the house and reset the alarm. They sat in the kitchen for a while with exhaustion and relief setting in equal measure. He brewed a cup of tea before suggesting they both needed some rest.

'It's been a long day. I think it's time for bed;' he suggested.
She nodded in agreement and then she said.
'I've not got a night dress. It's still packed in my luggage!'
'How about wearing a pair of my pyjamas?' he suggested.

She was too tired to object to his suggestion and when he brought down a set of his best silk pyjamas she excused herself to retire for the night. He had domestic matters to attend to so he kissed her and said good night. Having completed his chores he locked the outside door, switched off the downstairs lights and made his way upstairs to bed. Elizabeth's bedroom door was closed so he assumed she was asleep. He opened his door and was pleasantly surprised. She was sitting up in his bed wearing his pyjama top. He also noticed that the bottom half of his pyjamas were neatly folded at the bottom of the bed.

'I thought you were going back to the usual sleeping arrangement;' he said.

She laughed and stretched out her hands towards him and replied;

'I often wondered how comfortable this bed was. Now I know!'

# Chapter Ten

# A Family Crisis

When Michael slammed the phone down and cut short his call to his mother, he was angry particularly at the lecture from David. His wife, Margaret listened to the conversation and feared that his bad temper would spill over to her, so she quietly listened to his reaction to the call.

'Do you believe it, she called me a hypocrite because we lived together before we got married. She would not accept it was different from what she and her fancy man are doing now.'

'What's more she tells me now that Dad did not approve of us sharing my bedroom with you before we got married. I don't believe that, Dad never ever said anything to me. She does not seem to see that this guy she's got now could be in it for what he can get!'

'She is not poor. After Dad died she sold the family home and moved into her flat. The rest of the money went into her bank account. That is what he will be after. You know what that means? It means our inheritance will disappear if they get married.'

Margaret felt it was time to interrupt him and hopefully calm him down.

'Michael, it works two ways you know. Your Mum would inherit his money if they ever decided to get married. But it doesn't have to be like that. Don't you think your Mum would protect you in some way?' she reasoned.

'Not bloody likely if she decided to get married or any other stupid idea at her age!' he replied.

Nothing was going to change his mind about their relationship. To him, the memory of his father and his mother's part in that memory was too important. There was no room for that memory to be tarnished by accepting the presence of another man in his mother's life.
Margaret interrupted his thoughts.

'Darling you need to speak to your mother again. Your call must have upset her. Once the damage is done it's difficult to undo it. Why not call her again and try to;' she hesitated, 'to apologise!'

'Apologise! What do I have to apologise for?' he cried.

'She and her boyfriend should be apologising for causing so much upset!'

Margaret was beginning to understand the situation more logically than her husband, and her sympathy was now more inclined towards her mother in law. She needed to persuade her husband to change his position, but she didn't want to reignite his short temper.

'Michael, for once just take it calmly, it could be what you said over the phone that caused this upset. Look at it from your mother's point of view. She is getting on in years, she is a widow, living alone on her own. She has needs. Just think, one of us could be in her position someday. Your mother deserves to be happy and if she finds that happiness with another man then that is her business and we should be happy for her.'

'Go on, phone her and try to mend broken fences!' she added.

'I can't phone now. It's far too soon. I need to think things out. I will wait a day or two until she gets home;' he replied.

Michael recognised the reality of what his wife said, but he was not ready to accept that this was how it should be. Deep down in his mind he would never accept the presence of another man in his mother's life. She was the widow of his beloved father. He struggled with conflicting thoughts for two days before deciding to contact his mother again. But now he knew that his objective was to find some means of restoring the situation back to what it was before David arrived to disrupt his relationship with his mother.

Two days had passed since Elizabeth returned from her holiday with David. She was alone in her flat expecting a call from him. Any doubts she had about David or their relationship had gone. They had a wonderful holiday in Scotland and the joy she experienced on the night they arrived home had more or less convinced her that they were meant for each other. The loneliness she felt in her flat and the contrasting pleasure of his company in his home were praying on her mind. Big decisions were on the horizon. Although they had not discussed it, if he asked her to move into his place and sell the flat, she thought she would probably do it.

Her day dreaming about the future was interrupted by the telephone ringing. She picked up the receiver anticipating that it was David, but the caller spoke before she could acknowledge the call.

'Hello Mum. It's Michael here!'

She was surprised, unsure why he was calling so soon after his last call.

'Mum, I want to apologise for all the things I said last time we spoke.'

'Thank you Michael, I understand. It was partly my fault for not letting you know where I was. You must have been worried. We said very hurtful things but I forgive you and I hope you forgive me?'

So far, things were going according to the intention of his call to his mother so he continued.

'It has been a long time since we last met. Stephen has almost forgotten he has a Grandma. He is taking part in his school concert soon, so why don't you come down for that week and you can see him perform?'

Elizabeth suspected that her son was being devious and he was using her Grandson as emotional bait. She missed seeing Stephen. He had been a great joy to her during the years after the passing of her husband. She knew she had to accept the invitation, but she needed to talk to David first about the implications of this.

'I would love to come down. I have missed seeing Stephen and I wouldn't want to miss his concert. Let me have the date and I will come back to you tomorrow after I have checked a few things.'

He gave her the information, said he was looking forward to her visit and ended the call. She phoned David immediately to explain the situation with her son and her suspicions about the real motive behind the invitation.

'You can hardly refuse unless you can think up a really good reason for not going;' he advised.

She replied; 'I can't, at least not one that that would convince him. I know he is going to do his best to end our partnership but I have no idea how he hopes to succeed;'

David asked, 'Do you want me to come with you? I can stay in a hotel in London?'

'No! I don't think that would do any good. I just need to be strong and keep my temper and ignore his.'


David drove Elizabeth to Liverpool Lime Street Station and arrived with time to spare. They sat in the station café with a cup of coffee each. Conversation was awkward because of the visit and the unknown consequences of her meeting with her son. They finished their coffees and David took hold of her case and walked with her along the platform to find her carriage and the reserved seat by the window. Once she was seated he left the carriage and stood outside beside her window. As the train moved, he gave her a wave and whispered good luck. She put her fingers to her lips and then placed them on the window as a parting gesture.

The train picked up speed as it left the station on its way to Euston Station in London. Elizabeth sat back in her seat and tried to relax. In her heart she would have preferred to stay at home with David. But her maternal instincts towards her grandson compelled her to face up to whatever was in store. For the time being her son's motivation for the invitation was unknown. Her journey took just over two hours and she spent most of the time looking out of her window observing the ever changing scenery. When the train arrived at its destination she headed towards Fenchurch Street to complete her journey to Essex where her family lived. She did this journey so often in the past that she was quite at easy finding her way across London.

When she reached her final destination, she knew that their house was only a few streets away, so it was a pleasant opportunity to compose herself, also it was early afternoon and Michael would still be in his office in London. Margaret had confirmed that she would be at home to meet her. This was familiar territory to Elizabeth. During the earlier years of her marriage they lived nearby and were very happy there until her late husband's business required them to move away from Essex. It was ironic that their only son moved back to Essex after he graduated and married.

Margaret was there as promised and the warmth of her welcome surprised her. She had expected the normal cool reception. Stephen was still at school so they both settled down in the lounge and chatted. Their conversation was lively and Margaret asked lots of questions, particularly about David. How they meet? How did they get on? Was she happy, and so on. This was not what Elizabeth expected and she was beginning to feel there was an ally in the camp. Eventually Margaret did reveal her support and went so far as to disclose her husband's objective.

'Michael can be so unreasonable at times. Once he gets an idea into his head, he will not let it go. You probably know that he is set against anyone taking his Dad's place. That's really stupid but he just will not listen!' she paused and looked at Elizabeth.

'Do you know what he is after? she asked.

Elizabeth replied. 'I can make a number of guesses but I don't really know!'

'Well, for goodness sake don't say I told you but he wants you to sell your flat and move down her with us.'

It was out of character for Margaret to be so forth coming so Elizabeth felt she could be equally honest about her feelings.

'This is really kind of you because I did not know what to expect. I promise I will not say anything about what you have said. It's a kind thought but it would not work for me and I suspect it would not work for you!'

Margaret nodded her head in agreement then completely out of character she exclaimed. 'Sisterhood united!'

They both laughed and embraced to seal an unholy alliance.

Their conversation was interrupted by the arrival of Stephen from school. He rushed into the lounge with arms out stretched, 'Grandma!' he yelled. Thereafter all attention and conversation was centred around their family reunion. Margaret left them together to prepare their evening meal and await the arrival of her husband.

The doorbell rang and Stephen ran from the room to open the door for his father. The carefree atmosphere of the last hour changed as Michael was led into the room holding his son's hand.

'Look Dad! Grandma's here to stay with us.' he cried.

Michael moved towards his mother, embraced her and kissed both cheeks.

'It's good to see you Mum. Did you have a good journey?' he asked.

'Yes, it was fine. No holdups I'm glad to say.' she replied.

'How long are you here for?'

'I've got to leave on Thursday, because I have a medical appointment on Friday.'

'Nothing serious I hope?'

'No, it's just a routine appointment. My blood count is a bit low so they are carrying out some tests. Otherwise I am keeping quite well.' she replied.

'That's good! How is sunny Southport?'

Before she could reply Margaret announced that dinner was ready. They moved into the dining room where Michael opened a bottle of wine. He filled three glasses with wine and another with juice for his son. Then he proposed a toast.

'To you Mum and to family!'

She raised her glass sipped the wine and wondered if the toast was meant to exclude David from the family.

After the meal they returned to the lounge and watched the television with Stephen until it was time for him to go to bed. Elizabeth took this opportunity to say she was tired and blamed the journey as her excuse for an early night's sleep. Her bedroom was in a self contained annex with its own bathroom. Both she and her late husband slept there when they used to visit. She was happy that she would not intrude too much on the rest of the family. Once settled she phoned David to say that so far all had gone well. But she was more discrete this time to be sure that her call would not be overheard.

The following morning Michael left early for his daily commute into London. Stephen was ready to go to school before Elizabeth appeared for breakfast. Margaret worked part time at the school so she was on her own until Margaret returned after lunch. Elizabeth was pleased and relaxed at not having to confront her son for the time being.

Later that day Michael returned from his office and they sat down for their evening meal. There was no change to the family routine on account of their visitor. Most of the conversation centred on Stephen and the school concert the following day. His part in the concert was a solo piano performance, for which he was excited at the prospect of playing in front of an audience. His mother persuaded him to give his Grandma a demonstration on the family piano, which he did, much to her delight.

Stephen was sent off to bed and all three settled down in the lounge for the rest of the evening. There was a period of silence before Michael opened the conversation.

'You know Mum, we get worried at you living so far away from your family. If anything happened to you we wouldn't be there to help you.'

'You don't need to worry too much about that.' she replied. 'I'm quite able to look after myself and there is plenty of help at home if it was needed.'

She was thinking of David in that respect, but she was careful not to let her son think so.

'You are not getting any younger, what would happen, how would you cope if something serious happened like going into hospital?'

'That is not going to happen Michael, and if it did we would have to cross that bridge when it did!'

She was annoyed at the question but managed to keep her feelings in check.

Michael realised that this conversation was going nowhere. He promised Margaret that he would not mention his mother's affair and he promised he would keep his temper under control. So he came straight to the point.

'Margaret and I both think that you should pack up and move down here with us. You can move into the annex which has got all you need and you will be close to Stephen and make up for all the time you have lost being so far away from him.'

This was emotional blackmail and Elizabeth knew it. She knew that this offer would not work out in the long term and her son's real objective was to remove David from her life.

'That is really sweet of you both.' she replied. 'But I would just be a burden to both of you.'

'That's not true Mum, honestly we really want you to think about this;' he replied.

She took her time before replying. 'It might have worked out earlier just after your Dad passed away and I was on my own in our old house. That was a difficult time, but things are not so difficult now.'

She knew she was touching a sensitive issue and Michael knew it too. She knew that they never thought of making such an offer and were quite happy to leave her to sort her own life out because her needs did not fit in with theirs at that time. So she was determined to stick to her guns and resist her son's overtures.

Michael sensed he was loosing the argument. Her last remark awakened the guilt he felt then, when he and Margaret had seen his mother as a burden that would change their way of life and their ambitions. There was only one remaining question he could ask.

'So what is your future Mother?' Are you planning to get married or carry on as you are?'

Margaret spoke immediately 'Michael stop! That's not a question you should be asking your Mother. You promised not to do this.'

He was taken aback by his wife's intervention. He hoped indeed he expected she would support him. So he turned to his wife.

'We are family so it is a perfectly reasonable question to ask.'

But his wife's response was unexpected. 'It is not fair and it is none of our business until your Mum makes it so!'

Elizabeth was worried that she was becoming the subject of a family dispute so she interrupted them.

'You are right Margaret it is my business. As for your question Michael, I am not planning to get married and I do not know what you mean by 'carry on as you are!'

Margaret added to her response. 'Your Mum is happy with her life at the moment. Let's just be thankful for that.'

Michael relented, realising that he was taking on two formidable ladies who were supporting each other. He picked up his daily newspaper and retired to a corner of the room. Margaret looked at Elizabeth and shrugged her shoulders. Elizabeth acknowledged her by mouthing a silent thank you. The ladies settled down to watch the evening programmes on the television. Each knowing that they had achieved their own objectives.

Next day, Michael left early with the intention of returning in time to attend the school concert. The ladies went shopping in town, returning in time to meet Michael. They enjoyed the concert and were delighted with Stephen's performance. Afterwards, Michael suggested they should dine out and as a reward allow Stephen to decide the restaurant. So rather reluctantly they settled for an evening at Macdonald's.

Elizabeth was conscious that her son was rather cool towards her. He never mentioned last night's subject again and no mention had been made about David in any form what so ever. As she retired for the night she knew that certain matters had been left undone.

She awakened the following morning and packed her bag to be ready for the journey home. Margaret was sitting at the breakfast table but Michael had already left the house.

'Where is Michael?' Elizabeth asked.

'He has gone to work as usual.' Margaret replied.

'Why didn't he come in to say goodbye?'

'He said he didn't want to disturb you because you were sleeping.' Elizabeth let the matter pass. She was in time to see Stephen off to school then have a quick breakfast. She thanked Margaret for her support before saying goodbye and then she left to catch the train back to London.

On the train bound for Liverpool she had time to analyse the events of the past few days. Elizabeth concluded that she had established her relationship with David at the price of losing her son.

# Chapter Eleven

## His Father's Son

Michael Stewart left his home without saying goodbye to his mother. It was excuse enough that she was still asleep in her bedroom, but he now regretted his discourteous behaviour. As he walked towards his local train station, he collected his morning paper and then boarded his train bound for Fenchurch Street. This was his daily commuting routine. But today was different. His mind was awash with conflicting emotions. He was angry, confused and frustrated. This was all to do with his stubborn stance against his mother's association with another man.

Normally he would sit by the window of his carriage. He would unfold his newspaper and study the latest financial news in preparation for his daily work in the City. Today his paper lay folded on his lap and he was decidedly ill at ease. He wondered why he was so determined to thwart his mother's wishes and why was his father's memory his motivation for taking such a stance. As the train continued its journey and the carriage filled with commuters at each stop, he was oblivious to all that was happening around him. Distant memories filled his mind.

Michael was an only child. His parents Stephen and Elizabeth doted on the child and determined from an early age that they would do all they could to give him a good start in life. His mother was a school teacher, so a good education for her son was her priority. His father had graduated from university with honours. He was an ambitious civil servant who was being fast tracked to a higher grade in his department.

Michael progressed through primary school and at the age of eleven he achieved all that his parents had expected of him. His parents, encouraged by their son's academic potential, pursued and obtained a grant for their son that gave him a place in a good residential private school. Their hopes for Michael's education were thrown into doubt when his father was selected for further promotion. This was subject to him being willing to take up a vacant posting in a branch office in Liverpool. This career change caused many conflicting problems.

His mother gave up her teaching job on the understanding that she would find another appointment at their new location. They were content to sell their house and move up north, knowing that property was cheaper in Liverpool or in nearby locations. Eventually they decided to live in the seaside town of Southport because of its good commuting links with Liverpool.

Their biggest problem was their son and his best interests. If they had listened to their son, they would have known that he wanted to stay with his parents. Michael did not want to be left to board in a new school. His father had similar thoughts and was willing to sacrifice his son's private education to keep his family together. But his mother considered this a sacrifice too much and insisted Stephen's schooling should not be disrupted.

She was happy that suitable arrangements could be made for her son's welfare in their absence. During school holidays between terms Michael could stay in their new home in Southport. For the odd days when this would not be possible she knew that arrangements could be made for her son to stay with Michael's aunt, who had already agreed that her brother could stay there during his occasional meetings in London.

So, Michael was separated from his parents for the next six years except for occasional visits between school terms. During that time Michael had occasional contact with his father when he returned to London and they both stayed with his aunt. They shared the same room and a relationship developed that was much closer than his attachment to his mother. Unknown at the time, this was the start of an important change in his future family relationship.

Although Michael deeply resented his absence from a normal home life, he excelled academically at his boarding school and went on to a university in London where he studied for three years before graduating with honours. During that time he became more independent living in shared student accommodation. He still maintained regular contact with his father and was less inclined to visit the family home in Southport. His mother, who was still teaching, managed occasional visits to London with her husband. They stayed in hotels, but her contacts with her son were less personal.

One of the students staying in the accommodation was Margaret. She and Michael became attached to each other and in due course became partners living together. Michael's father was fairly relaxed about their relationship but Elizabeth was less happy and this led to a degree of disapproval between her and Margaret.

Michael's academic achievements enabled him to find employment in the booming financial services market in the City. In time he and Margaret married and they had a son called Stephen after his grandfather. Michael progressed in his job and they were able to purchase a property in Essex close to where Michael was born. His mother and father became regular visitors to their home which had ample space to accommodate them. His father also stayed there when he was required to attend to his business London.

Then one day tragedy struck. Elizabeth's husband suddenly died. At the time he was staying with his family in their home in Essex. He collapsed with a severe heart attack. Michael was unable to help his father before medical assistance arrived. He was left traumatised by the experience and with a lasting feeling of guilt. His mother never knew the exact circumstances of her husband's death and Michael never discussed this with her. By subconsciously transferring the guilt to his mother, it relieved his own guilt caused by the circumstances of his father's death. Why?

Many years ago when his mother insisted he should go to boarding school against his and his father's wishes was a crossroad in Michael's life. Hidden deep in Michael's mind, this chain of events resulting in his father's death led back to that fateful decision made by his mother.

Michael's morning journey into London ended at Fenchurch Street Station. He was no further able to resolve his confused thoughts. Outwardly, he was unable to rationalise his antagonism towards his mother. But the answer lay deep in his subconscious mind.

# Chapter Twelve

## A Daughter's Blessing

While Elizabeth was visiting her son, David thought it would be opportune to have another heart to heart talk with his daughter Julie. The last time they talked about 'his lady friend' was when the family stayed during the anniversary of her mother's death. He was in two minds whether to invite the family to come to him or to invite him self to their home. If he chose the latter he would have to stay overnight in a hotel because there was not enough room in their house. He had good reason for choosing this option.

When Clare was alive she coped with the chaos that accompanied a family visit, and she shielded him from the results. It was an entirely different matter now that he was on his own. As well as the aftermath of stripping beds, laundering linen and towels and restoring the household back to normality, he found their domestic routines hard to understand. The children seemed to think that the normal place for things that left their hands was the floor. It annoyed him to be continually picking things up afterwards. Evening conversations were severely limited because the parents and children were individually and collectively obsessed with their mobile phones. For hours they sprawled around his lounge staring into these small devices, the only detectable sign of life being the flicking of a thumb or frantic tapping on the illuminated screen. Invariably he was left to look at an unwatched television and wonder why they had bothered to come. So, without further ado he picked up the phone and announced he would be making an overnight stay in two days time. Fortunately for him his visit was welcomed by Julie.

Julie, her husband and the twins Susan and Jane lived in the north east of England in Gateshead. They lived in a terraced house close to the banks of the river Tyne. The house was too small for her growing family and when she tried to persuade her father to move, she secretly hoped he might be persuaded to buy a house large enough for all the family to live together. She knew that was not possible knowing his attachment to Elizabeth, so she was hopeful that his visit might clarify his position.

Julie worked as a nurse at the local hospital. Her shift rota fitted in with the day of her father's arrival. Her husband James used to work in an engineering factory in the town but was made redundant two years ago and now took charge of the domestic duties while Julie's salary was the main source of income. Things had been difficult for them for a long time and David and his late wife Clare periodically helped them in times of need.

He set off in his car early in the morning hoping to get there by lunch time. A reservation was made for an overnight stop at a nearby travel lodge. He booked in and left his car there and took the short walk to his daughter's home. She was waiting there to greet him. They embraced and Julie ushered him into her tiny living room where her husband James was waiting. They sat down with a welcome cup of tea and Julie opened the conversation.

'It's great to see you again Dad, but why the short notice and why are you going home again tomorrow?'

'Sorry dear, there are things I need to talk to you both about and I didn't want to do it over the phone.'

'Why? Are things all right with you?' she asked.

'I'm fine. There are no problems with me or the house. It's more personal than that.'

Julie glanced at her husband because they had speculated that the reason for the visit was something to do with his involvement with Elizabeth. When she first heard that they went off on a holiday to Scotland together and alone she was shocked although her husband had regarded it as a more acceptable occasion. But she concealed her true feelings consoled by the thought if her father was happy then she was happy too.

David spoke first. 'You know all about Elizabeth and you liked her. Well, we have become a lot closer recently and I felt it was time to keep you in the picture.'

'What do you mean by getting closer Dad? You are not thinking of getting married again, are you?' she asked.

'No, no! It's not about that. It's just that we have become - what's the modern term? We have become - an Item!'

James chuckled and without much thought he exclaimed.

'What? Like something on a shopping list?'

His joke was not well received and he slunk back into his seat.

David continued. 'You know that we went on holiday. Since then we have become very close. You know Elizabeth really helped me to overcome the depression I had after your Mum died. I'm grateful to her for that and I'm a lot happier now and she is happy too.'

Julie hesitated for a moment. She was lost for the right words.

'How would Mum feel about this?' she asked.

'If Mum was here this would not have happened!' he quickly replied.

'If Mum's looking down now, I think she would be happy for my sake!'

Julie realised she had touched a delicate spot and she knew that he was upset by the question. She immediately responded.

'Dad I am here and I can speak on Mum's behalf. We are happy for you and we give you our blessings. Now let's have the rest of your good news.'

The rest of the afternoon passed quickly and Julie was now content that her father and Elizabeth were indeed an Item and she was looking forward to meeting her again. Their conversation was broken by the arrival of his grand children from school. School bags were dropped on the floor, school blazers were carelessly thrown over a chair and the girls, with their mobile phones firmly gripped in their hands rushed over to greet their Grandpa. James prepared a light evening meal and Julie got dressed for her night duty at the hospital. After the meal, David readied himself to return to the travel lodge. Just before he left he had one more thing to say to his daughter. He waited until they left the house together.

'There is just one more thing dear. I didn't mention this earlier. You know your Mum had a will and I have one now? Mum and I arranged that if one of us went first the other would be the main beneficiary. If and when both of us went then our wills stated that you would inherit whatever was left. I want you to know that whatever happens between me and Elizabeth, your Mum's wish will not change. That's my promise to you!'

Julie walked with her father to his lodgings. She was lost for words. What her father said upset her. Never had she thought about the consequences of her father's will and the possible implications of having a future step mother. She had benefited from her mother's will in a small way but she could not comprehend the consequences of being a sole beneficiary under these circumstances.

'Dad, I don't really want to know about this. It was bad enough when Mum died.
I could not bear to go through it again. So promise me you are going to live forever!'

'Her father took her hand. 'Listen dear, that is something I would not wish on anyone. You have to be strong when that time comes.'
She had a tear in her eye as they embraced each other.

'Goodbye Dad, I love you.' she whispered and set of to the hospital.

The day after Elizabeth returned home she attended her appointment. The medical staff carried out their routine checks and tests but they were unable or perhaps reluctant to come to any conclusion before the tests were analysed. She made another appointment to return in six months. Any concerns she had about her health were put to one side. Instinctively she was content to wait rather than worry prematurely about the possibility of an unwelcome diagnosis.

When they got together again they were pleased to get back into their interrupted routines. Their first social occasion was to attend an evening performance at the Little Theatre. They sat in the bar before the start. The place was busy, mostly with strangers but one or two faces were familiar. Suddenly David was startled from behind by a hand on his shoulder. He turned round to greet a colleague from his working days.

'Good lord Bill, I haven't seen you since my retirement party! How are you doing?'

'I am fine. My retirement date is coming up soon so I am looking for good advice on how to make the most of it.' Bill replied.

He turned to look at Elizabeth and David introduced her.

'Meet Elizabeth, we are good friends. We have been friends since Clare, my wife passed away.'

Bill was slightly embarrassed because he was unaware that Clare had died. He said

'I am really sorry to hear about Clare. I didn't know this had happened. But I am pleased to meet you Elizabeth. You make a smashing couple.'

He slapped David on the shoulder.

'Now I know who to come to for some post retirement advice!'

David looked at Elizabeth with raised eyebrows in silent disapproval of what might have seemed like an innocent remark. She too recognised it as having an unwelcome double meaning. The final call to go to the auditorium changed their moods and they spent the rest of the evening enjoying the play.

Elizabeth had agreed to stay with David that evening after the show, so they settled down for a glass of wine before retiring for the night. They chatted for a while recalling some of the events arising from their visits. Both were content that Michael was aware of their position and

Elizabeth was now at ease with his continuing opposition. But she then raised one thing that Michael said that still left doubts in her mind.

'When Michael was trying very hard to break us apart he asked me a question. He asked me…was I getting married or carrying on as we were?'

'What did you say?' asked David.

'I got angry and told him it was none of his business. But it was a fair question and I was angry because I didn't know how to answer.'

'Maybe we should try and find an answer!' he suggested.

'Well let's talk about it;' she replied.

They both accepted that the question was completely relevant to their situation. Their future relationship had two possible outcomes covered by her son's question. Either they got married or they continued as partners with the opportunity of maintaining separate lives. They talked deep into the night and in the end they came to an understanding without reaching a positive conclusion. Both agreed that marriage should have been the only decision for a loving couple, irrespective of age. But they accepted it was a selfish decision. Too many obstacles were in the way. They had to consider the impact it would have on the families. Then there were the personal decisions of merging two households and the gains and losses that would entail. In the end they agreed that a loving partnership was the most logical and least disruptive option left. It was not the committal they would have wished to make.

Now they were left with finding a way to make their partnership work. Straight away they had to confront a serious problem. Both agreed that their intermittent living arrangements were unsatisfactory. Ideally they wanted to live permanently together. It was not practical for him to move into her flat. She would willingly move into his house and be happy there. A third option, although unlikely was for both to sell their homes and find somewhere else to live.

The obvious answer was for Elizabeth to move into David's home. But what could she do about her flat? She knew that would reignite opposition from her son and it would be a great matter of trust on her part if their relationship broke down. David understood this. He would not expect her to carry all the risks for a partnership that could not provide the security of a proper commitment through marriage. He was also mindful of the promise he gave to his daughter.

They reluctantly concluded that for the time being they would conduct their lives together more or less as they were.

## Chapter Thirteen

## Come Back to Sorrento

For the time being a final solution to their partnership was put to one side. They were very happy with things as they were. Most of their friends and acquaintances accepted them as a normal couple in a marital state for all intents and purposes. They had no concern for the silent few, who for their own reasons, frowned upon the intimacy of their relationship.

Elizabeth now spent quality time staying with David. She loved the freedom of space and the ability to find a quiet spot when needed. She loved the garden, the opportunity to tend to the plants and relax in a secluded spot. Most of all she loved the birds that visited the feeding boxes and the nesting habits of the Blue Tits. All of this contrasted with the confinement of her flat. She would have gladly sacrificed the community spirit of her place for the sense of freedom missing in her life since her husband died. But she could not neglect the need to maintain the flat so her extended visits to his home were limited.

One thing she did during these visits, not always to David's liking, was to restore the woman's touch. The vases were now filled with fresh flowers and opened windows removed the stuffy still air he was used to. The dressing table in the bedroom now had an array of cosmetics and other ladies essentials. She was not adverse to shifting him from his comfortable chair as she vacuumed his lounge carpet. In truth, he was delighted because she was restoring life into what was a lonely home.

David visited Elizabeth's flat less frequently. He helped with the occasional odd job and decorating was well within his ability. But he never stayed overnight. Her bedroom was small and they both agreed that any intimate sleeping arrangement would be less than ideal. However he did enjoy visits when she would cook a lunch or a dinner just for them. She was more at ease in her own kitchen and more adventurous with the quality and variety of her menus.

Elizabeth was always keen that he should meet Grace, her next door neighbour. She had formed a close bond with Grace, ever since she moved into the flat and they provided mutual support when ever it was needed. So one day she introduced Grace to David and to her great delight their first meeting went well. Elizabeth confided that Grace held a spare key for her flat and Grace was content to let David know that her spare key was held by Elizabeth. So he was now recruited into a mutual support group of three.

At times, particularly at home in the evenings, they would have moments of quiet reflection. They knew they were blessed to be able to enjoy a friendship that enhanced their quality of life. But this was a twilight love affair and they knew it. They knew and accepted that their time together could be counted at best in years, certainly not in decades. At their time of life they accepted that their future was uncertain and in time they would follow nature's laws and make way for their next generation.

Elizabeth felt this anxiety more strongly than David. For a long time her general health was not what it should be. She was very adept at hiding her feelings, particularly to David. She could maintain a normal disposition even when her body was telling her otherwise. Her routine health checks and periodic blood tests were not causing alarm and she was less interested in following up the results with her surgery. She had no wish to have any medical intervention interfere with the contentment of her present relationship with David.

They successfully weathered their second winter together and warmth was returning to the springtime weather. Their thoughts were now turning to an early holiday together. The social club was planning a group holiday to Bournemouth but that was later in the year. They were interested in something sooner. The unlimited choices available made it all the more exciting. They scoured the weekend newspapers with their holiday supplements and they picked up travel brochures from travel agents and searched the internet for bargain offers.

One morning their search was interrupted by the rattling of David's letter box. This heralded the arrival of the morning post which he went to retrieve. He returned with a single brown envelope. It was a letter from the Council which he opened and quietly read its contents. Suddenly he exclaimed:

'Bloody hell! Listen to this.' He began to read to Elizabeth.

'It has come to our attention that the conditions for sole tenancy of the above property may no longer apply. You are reminded that the 25% discount on the rateable value of this property ceases with the end of sole tenancy and you have a duty to inform the Council accordingly .....'

'What does all that mean?'.

'It means that some bloody interfering busybody thinks they can blow the whistle on me!' he replied.

'Who would do such a things?' she asked.

'It could be anybody, a neighbour, a not so friendly friend. Anyone who wants to cause me mischief!'

There was a contact number in the letter so he phoned straight away. He confirmed the second person implied by the letter was a visitor and not a resident. The person at the other end of the phone was not fully accepting this explanation and David was becoming irritated by the questioning.

'Look! I know five hundred pounds is a lot of money but I am not depriving the Council of anything. The second person you keep referring to happens to have her own property and she pays her Council Tax in the same way as me! What more proof do you need?'

That seemed to settle the issue and he replaced the receiver.

'It goes to show you, we don't always know who is for and whose against us.'

With the distraction over, they returned to the travel brochures and finally agreed that an Italian holiday would do just nicely. What's more it was going to be a romantic week in a good hotel in Sorrento.

They flew into Naples and were met by a courier who directed them on to a waiting coach to take them and others on to Sorrento. The hotel was all they dreamed of, perched on a steep cliff top overlooking the Bay of Naples. They had their first sighting of the outline of Mount Visuvius just inland of the Bay. The room was spacious with a wide balcony facing the Bay. A small bottle of Italian wine and fresh fruit lay on a table as a welcoming gift from the hotel manager. There was just one flaw in the arrangements, they looked at the two single beds and laughed. This was a new sleeping arrangement and David jokingly commented.

'Well we should get some good nights sleep!'

Elizabeth was not amused but she could not disagree with his sentiment.

They changed out of their travelling clothes and readied themselves for their first evening meal in the hotel. Tables were set on the outside veranda and they were led to a table with a clear view of the Bay. The sun was setting over the sea, illuminating the outline of Mount Visuvius. The lights of Naples and the coastal towns gradually appeared like a string of pearls garlanding the coastline. The waiter lit the candle on their table and the scene was set for a memorable first night in Sorrento.

After their leisurely meal they returned to their room. They sat in the balcony with a warm breeze gently blowing the curtains behind them. They could hear the distant chatter of guests having a late meal in the restaurant below. The outline of the surrounding hills and the volcano were barely visible against the dark sky, but they were surprised to see so many distant lights on the lower slopes. They listened to the gentle ripple of water lapping against the harbour and they were at peace with their world. Finally, the effects of their long journey and a fine bottle of wine caught up with them and they retired to their single beds with an undeclared satisfaction with their new sleeping arrangements.

The early morning sounds of the town and harbour coming to life wakened them from a sound sleep. The routine procedures for the bathroom caused some unexpected embarrassment for Elizabeth but eventually that was dealt with and they were dressed and ready for breakfast and the first full day of the holiday. After breakfast they were invited to an introductory meeting with their tour guide. She presented a number of options, all being equally inviting. Elizabeth chose a coach trip to the Amalfi coast and David wanted to go to the summit of Vesuvius and they both agreed that a visit to the ruins of Pompii was a must. Having paid for the organised trips they spent the rest of the day exploring Sorrento and the harbour where they watched the regular departure of boats taking tourists to the Isle of Capri. They hoped to be able to fit this trip into their busy schedule.

A small restaurant near the harbour caught their attention and they sat in the shade away from the sun, sipping Peronni beer and enjoying a typical Italian pasta lunch. Later on they found shelter in the town's museum where the air conditioning provided welcome relief from the afternoon sun. Suitably refreshed, window shopping became Elizabeth's priority. This was of little interest to David until he found a side alley that led to a large fronted shop and workshop. They were fascinated with the window display of beautifully crafted and decorated musical boxes. They joined other visitors inside the shop who were viewing the craftsmen at work in their workshop. Elizabeth was entranced by the whole scene. She picked a box from the display, turned it over and read the small label which read; *Torna a Surriento*. She opened the lid and was completely captivated by the tone and quality of the music. David noted her delight and took careful note of the box she was holding.

The Sorrento Peninsula forms the southern arm of the Bay and the Amalfi coastal road snakes along the south side of the Peninsula. The road follows the contours of the cliff edge. So, they were careful to sit on the right hand side of the coach to benefit from the unrestricted sea views. Those who sat on the opposite side of the coach were less fortunate with only the vertical cliff wall to view. The cliff edge dropped vertically down to the sea and as they approached their destination they were surprised to see the occasional villa or restaurant precariously perched on the edge of the cliff. It was a picturesque journey finishing with a winding descent into the beautiful town of Positano nestling between the cliffs and the sea. They spent a pleasant few hours exploring the narrow streets and enjoyed a meal in a café overlooking the sea. Their homeward journey took them inland, much to the disappointment of the fellow travellers on the opposite side of the coach.

They returned to the hotel late in the afternoon and retired to their room to recover from their tiring journey. They agreed for the need of a shower, each offering the other first option. After a few moments of indecision David looked at Elizabeth and said. 'Hell, we're on holiday, let's share the shower. It's big enough for two!'
Initially she was taken aback by his outrageous suggestion, but replied.
  'This could be embarrassing but let's give it a try!'

They quickly changed into their dressing gowns. Hand in hand they walked into the shower room. The walls were covered in decorative Italian tiles and the floor sloped slightly towards an open shower. He ran the water and asked if she wanted it to be cold.

'Not too cold!' she replied.

He hung his dressing gown on a hook and with his hand covering a strategic part of his anatomy he stepped under the shower, recoiling from the initial shock of the cold water.

'Come on in, it's lovely!' he cried

She put a bathing cap on to cover her hair, dropped her gown and followed him into the shower. He moved over to let her feel the full force of the water. She got used to the cold water and quickly abandoned her bathing cap to let her hair fall freely under the water. They realised that the best way to share the full force of the shower was to stand close together, and soon they were in a close embrace. Their hands ran freely around each other without embarrassment. David reached for a small bottle of shower gel and gently massaged the soap onto her body, exploring hidden parts as he went on. Elizabeth did likewise and they lingered under the refreshing water like small children without embarrassment or shame.

This was a new experience for them and not without its problems. But they got into the swing of things and both had a lot of fun. The rest of the afternoon passed peacefully with both quietly napping on their beds until the evening air cooled the room and another dinner on the veranda awaited them.

The next day they visited the ancient ruins of Pompii. The site was full of tourists, all entranced by the scale of destruction yet impressed by the orderly way in which it had been excavated. Elizabeth recalled her experience in Scotland and kept wondering what stories lay hidden in the ruined walls that surrounded her. Evidence of wall paintings in some buildings reinforced her thoughts on the magic of stone. They came to a large open area and there in the distance they saw for the first time the juxtaposition of the ruins and the source of its destruction, the still active Mount Visuvius. The volcano erupted over 2000 years ago and they could not contemplate the terror of that destruction until they saw for the first time, the plaster casts of bodies found where they died all these years ago. David was more eager than ever to climb to the top of Mount Visuvius.

That opportunity came two days later when they went on their last organised tour. The road from Sorrento to Naples weaved along the coast, hugging the high cliff edge in places. As they approached Naples the scene changed to a bustling city, with narrow streets and the chaos of vehicles competing with motor cyclists and pedestrians to occupy the limited capacity of the roads. To the right, the menacing slopes of Vesuvius filled the skyline. Their coach approached the lower slopes and travelled around the mountain to climb a winding road leading closer to the summit. They passed through the solidified lava field looking grey and menacing as a reminder of ancient eruptions. What was more incredulous was the sight of habitation on these slopes.

The volcano was over 3900 feet high but the road allowed their coach to park closer to the summit. But that left a formidable climb up a steep winding path to be travelled before reaching the summit. David had no doubts about the task and although Elizabeth was less keen she reluctantly agreed to accompany him. They reached the rim of the crater and to Elizabeth's horror she could see small whiffs of steam or smoke, she didn't know which, coming from fissures at the far side of the crater. The volcano clearly was not dormant and she felt uneasy. David turned her attention away from the rim to look out towards the sea and the sprawling city and surrounding suburbs reaching the foothills below.

He had done his homework so he was able to impress her with some facts. 'Do you know there are over three million people living down there and the last time it erupted was in 1944 and they reckon it erupted fifty times before then. So in all probability it's going to erupt again. I read somewhere that this was just the tip of a giant cauldron of underground seas of molten lava deep down beneath our feet

That's unthinkable!' he cried.

Elizabeth was quite unnerved by now and greatly relieved to return to the comfort of the coach.

This was a truly wonderful holiday for the couple. To finish it off on their last free day they wandered down to the harbour and booked passage to the romantic Isle of Capri. This was a holiday they would remember for the rest of their days. It finished all too quickly and they were left with fond memories of their experiences in Italy.

The day after they returned from the holiday, David visited Elizabeth in her flat. She had prepared lunch and he was anxious to meet again. He brought a small package which he gave to her.

'This is my present to you as a reminder of our holiday in Sorrento;' he said, kissing her on the lips.

She looked at the package and was genuinely surprised because she was not aware of him buying anything like this when they were together. She opened the package and her eyes lit up immediately. She was delighted. It was the musical box she last saw in Sorrento. She opened the lid of the box and it played a song most fitting for this occasion. It played; *Come Back to Sorrento.* She cried and embraced David tightly. Then she noticed something else in the box, three small lumps of stone. 'What's this?' she asked.

'Three pieces of pumice volcanic rock I picked up on Visuvius;' he replied.

She took the stones from the box, cradled them in her hand and sighed.

'Now these are stones that do have a story to tell!'

# Chapter Fourteen

## To Be or Not to Be

Three years have passed since David's wife Clare died. His daughter Julie and her family were staying with him for their annual visit to remember her. Elizabeth was now an accepted member of the family and was particularly pleased now that the twins Susan and Jane called her Auntie Liz. She slept in her own flat during the family visit, as a matter of convenience to allow his family to stay under the one roof. Julie took over the domestic duties during her stay and she prepared a special lunch to which Elizabeth was invited.

Elizabeth joined Julie in the kitchen. Although they had met a number of times this was the first time they were alone and both were eager to get to know each other more. Elizabeth opened the conversation.
'Have you settled into your new home?'
'Yes thank you;' she replied. 'It's really good to have a bigger house. The girls have their own bedrooms now and they love it.'
'I am so pleased your Dad was able to help you.'
'Yes without his help it would have been impossible to get a mortgage. Not only that, he helped James to get back into work and

now he is doing quite well as a self employed handyman so we are coping nicely.'

Julie was anxious to change the discussion so she asked about Elizabeth's health.

'What about you?' Last time we met you were having trouble with headaches.'

'I am still taking the tablets!' she replied. 'But I just get on with it. I am supposed to have regular checkups but nothing ever changes. So, I try not to bother too much anymore. My repeat medical prescriptions keep me going!' she replied.

Julie was surprised at this and replied; 'Speaking as a nurse now, you should be taking the checkups more seriously. If there is something affecting your health that is the only way they can find the cause and prescribe the best treatment.'

Elizabeth nodded in agreement, but intuitively she did not really want to know for fear of hearing an unwelcome result. They fell silent for a few moments to concentrate on the tasks at hand before Julie raised another topic of interest to her.

'Are you quite happy with your relationship with Dad?' she asked. ' I mean would you not like to get married now?'

Elizabeth was cautious about replying. 'Complications! Complications!' she replied.

'What complications? That's nonsense, replied Julie.

'We talked about it a lot in the beginning but your Dad felt it would be unfair on the families. So that is how it has been and is likely to continue. Although from my point of view being married to your Dad would be ever so good.'

'Honestly, I would love to be able to call you Step Mother.'

'That's really sweet of you, best to ask your Dad.'

'I will! I am going to see what I can do about that!' replied Julie

The food was now ready so their conversation finished and the ladies efforts turned to serving lunch to the hungry family waiting patiently in the dining room. After their meal was over conversation got round to the matters discussed in the kitchen. Julie started the ball rolling by addressing her father directly.

'Dad, how long have you and Elizabeth been together?'

'It's coming up for three years;' he replied.

'Don't you think it was about time you got married?'

He replied, 'We did think about it at the beginning but we felt that our family commitments made marriage too difficult and we didn't think you would approve.'

'That's not true, there is no reason why we should object, if it would make you both happy.' she replied.

'Well we felt that if any one of us passed away it would lead to a lot of difficulties with inheritance and all that stuff.' David replied.

'Oh Dad! .That's an awful excuse for not doing the right thing.'

Turning towards Elizabeth she said; 'Go ahead. Do it! ... I'll be your bridesmaid Elizabeth!'

And I'm available as your best man Pop!' added James.

David looked at Elizabeth and with a rueful smile asked. 'Have you two been cooking up more than the lunch in the kitchen?'
The ensuing laughter provided him with the perfect opportunity to avoid giving a direct answer. But clearly marriage was now on the agenda and at the appropriate time it would be discussed once again. For the moment, the lingering memory of his late wife meant that now was not the time for that discussion.

They spent the rest of the day quietly at home. David, Julie and James sat in the lounge watching the television whilst Elizabeth had happily volunteered to the request of the twins to read a story from their favourite book. Elizabeth was not just a guest here. She felt at home and part of David's family.

Unhappily for her, the same relationship did not exist with her own family. Her son had almost cut her out of his life. Time had not healed his objection to her affair with David and the disrespect he felt she had for the memory of his father. Her only contact with her family came from his wife, Margaret. They spoke on the telephone at times when Michael was not at home. Occasionally she managed to speak to her grandson Stephen after he came home from school. It distressed her that Stephen was becoming less interested in talking to her. The intimate bond between a grandparent and child was loosening because of her absence. He was growing up and she was a relative stranger with less and less in common with the interests of a young boy. She would dearly love to visit them to reverse this situation, but no such invitation came or was likely.

Because her relations with her family had drifted so far apart, they now took second place to her relationship with David and her developing affection for his family. Although she hated the thought, the reasons for not marrying David were of less significance to her. She could not say that to him partly because she was ashamed at the thought of it and partly because he seemed content with their present situation.

David's family left for home the following day and Elizabeth arrived shortly after, having agreed to help him restore the house to normality after the departure of his loving but exceeding untidy family.

'Thanks for helping me out;' he said. 'This house is a bloody mess! Look at this, sweet wrappers stuffed down the sofa. As much as I love them they are an untidy bunch. Towels on the bathroom floor - dishes unwashed - beds left unmade. No wonder I don't want to go and live with them!'

Elizabeth replied, 'You are an old fuss pot, you loved every minute they were here!'

'I have to thank you,' he answered.

'Why?

'For a start, you managed to keep the twins away from their mobile gadgets for a while and we had meaningful conversations for once. We managed to talk about the problem of us getting married.'

Elizabeth added. 'I was surprised at how keen Julie was for us to get married.'

'Ah yes, I think there was a little bit of female conspiracy going on there was there not?' he replied.

'Maybe, but we didn't get a positive response from you, did we?'

'Well it was not the right time to talk about it with the anniversary, and all that.' he replied.

'Is the time right now? she asked.

'Well nothing has really changed has it? The complications we talked about in the beginning are still there. Julie's approval will not change anything when the time comes and it's not going to help you with Michael. It will only make a bad situation worse.'

She was disappointed by his lack of interest but could only agree with his conclusion. Their present relationship, despite its shortcomings was best for the time being, but could it last?

All the domestic chores were complete and the house was back to normality. They had time now to sit down with a warm cup of tea and think about all that happened over the last few days and contemplate what lay ahead knowing that a more permanent and desirable option of marriage was unlikely in the foreseeable future.

Elizabeth broke the silence. 'I was so happy over the last few days. I felt like one of the family. Julie was just like the daughter I always wanted, and the twins! We really bonded and how sweet to be called Auntie Liz! They made me realise how much I missed with my own grandson.'

Tears filled her eyes and David moved closer to be beside her. He put his arms around her and held her tightly. She placed her head on his shoulder and wept immersed in her inner thoughts.

## Chapter Fifteen

## Decision Time

The sands of time were running out and their relationship was changing. Elizabeth's bouts of ill health were making things difficult at times. She was finding more reasons to deal with her problems in the solitude of her flat. She found her neighbour Grace an alternative source of support during these times.

They still led a normal social life together but more often than not she preferred to finish the day at home rather than staying with David. He was conscious of the gradual changes that were taking place. He knew that her health problems were a contributory factor so he never openly questioned her decisions. In truth, he had his own health problems and he too appreciated the occasional release of responsibility towards her. So, a gradual but mutually acceptable change in the intimacy of their affair developed. Perhaps it was an inevitable outcome of their rejection of marriage as a more solid foundation for sharing their lives together.

This change in their relationship worried David. He missed the regular contact with her, especially the intimacy of her presence in his home and how she played such an important part in his life. He was conscious of a return of periods of depression during her absence, much as it was before he met her. In his darkest moments he worried that it might lead to early signs of dementia. This filled him with dread, knowing how badly it affected his late wife, He knew that being with Elizabeth put all his fears to one side and he knew now that something needed to be done to revive what was now in danger of being lost.

He picked up the phone to speak to her to suggest that they meet the following day and go out somewhere special. Elizabeth willingly agreed and it was arranged that they would meet at her flat the following morning.

It was a sunny spring morning as David parked his car outside Elizabeth's flat. They had agreed to go out for the day to Lytham St Anne's on the Lancashire coast. This was her favourite location so David was anticipating a happy occasion. He arrived early so he switched of the engine and was admiring the spring flowers at front of the building when the front door of the flat opened. It was not Elizabeth as he expected but Grace her next door neighbour. He waved and got out of his car to go and speak to her.

'Good morning Grace, how are you today?'

'Hello Mr Fulton, are you waiting for Elizabeth?' she replied.

'Please call me David. Yes we are going out for the day, but I'm a bit early, off shopping are you?'

'I'm just going down the road to pick up a few things.'

She paused and moved towards David.

'David, I get worried about Elizabeth. She is not her usual self these days and her health worries me. You know, the walls in these flats are not exactly sound proof and I hear her getting up at night a lot. She needs someone to look after her!'

With her last emphatic statement she was off to do her shopping.

He returned to his car to wait for Elizabeth. Grace's last statement shocked him with its obvious truth. Suddenly his mind cleared. He realised his concerns about the consequences of getting married also had consequences for not getting married. He now knew what needed to be done.

His thoughts were interrupted as Elizabeth appeared at the front door. She looked pale but still attractive in her summer attire.

'Sorry I'm late dear. I didn't have a very good night.'

That's okay. We are not in any hurry. The sea air at Lytham will blow away your cobwebs.'

He settled her in the car and drove out of the car park heading for a new day. He drove north along the coast road past the dormant Pleasureland fairground and the Ocean Plaza leisure complex. The tide was out and the sea was nowhere to be seen. They passed the long car park with its memories of a brief encounter with the police. Soon they were on the main road heading towards Preston. They bypassed the city centre and soon they were heading towards Blackpool before turning off towards their destination.

She was enjoying the changing scenery and he was rehearsing in his mind how he intended to convey his intentions to her. Finally they arrived. He drove into the town along the coastal road and parked the car close to the town's famous windmill

'This should do us for four hours.' He fumbled for change for the parking meter.

'That's lovely, it gives us plenty of time for a walk along the front, a spot of lunch and a bit of shopping.' she replied.

'Sounds good!' he agreed.

They held hands as they walked along the promenade. The tide was out and the refreshing breeze invited a brisk walk. After a while he suggested they rest on a bench to admire the sea view looking out towards Southport in the distant end of the bay. The place was quiet with only a few people nearby exercising their dogs.

David turned towards Elizabeth and clasped both her hands.

He said, 'I want to talk to you about something important.'

At first she was apprehensive, fearing the worst, but she could hear in his voice and see in his eyes that this was something different.

'Before you came down this morning I was talking to Grace. She said something that was very important to me.'

Elizabeth asked. 'What did she say?'

'She said I should look after you, but what I think she meant was that we should look after each other.'

Elizabeth was momentarily lost for words. She was not quite sure what he meant so she paused to allow him to continue.

'Elizabeth, I think we should get married. Will you marry me?'
She squeezed his hands and leant forward to kiss him with all the passion she could muster.

'I will! I will!' she cried.

They embraced for a while until they were distracted by a passing elderly couple walking their dog. The couple smiled, greeted them and went on their way.. Elizabeth now wondered why this sudden change of mind. So she asked him;

'When we get married, what about all these consequences that worried you?'

'To hell with the consequences!' he exclaimed.

'There are consequences if we don't get married and they are more important to us. Our life together is too short to worry about that now. We need to do what is best for us and that is to get married.'

They celebrated their special occasion by treating themselves to an expensive lunch in one of the many restaurants in the town. To complete the day and seal their intentions, David insisted on buying her an engagement ring. They found a jeweller's shop on the main street where he hoped to find a ring that would please her.

'Not too expensive!' declared Elizabeth.

The assistant produced two trays full of suitable engagement rings. Elizabeth tried one on her left hand. It was a good fit and David nodded his approval. He produced his credit card and the ring was placed in a box and then gift wrapped. He put the package in his jacket pocket.

'We're not engaged yet!' he said.

'We will find a time and place to our liking to make our engagement official.

Elizabeth embraced him, took his arm and said.

'Roll on that happy, happy day!'

They passed the remainder of the day sitting in the park. The late afternoon sun had brought families out and they enjoyed watching the children at play. David lightly tapped the pocket of his jacket containing the ring. He held her hand and said.

'Now this is going to seal our love for each other and nobody in the whole world can deny us.'

Elizabeth smiled. But in her heart she knew there was one person who could deny them that right. That person was her own son, and even at this late stage in their affair it caused her great distress. By the time they got back to the car park they had exceeded their time but fortunately there was no parking ticket.

They arrived back in Southport after a long but eventful day. Elizabeth invited David back to her flat for a light evening snack to finish off their day. He agreed and was now hopeful that today's events would revitalise their relationship and that he would indeed be able to look after her. They sat in the lounge and talked about planning the engagement and the wedding. By the end of the evening they agreed it would be better to be married in the Registry Office and to have a modest reception for family and a few friends. Finally the question of a honeymoon came up. Before he could say a word she moved over to her display cabinet and lifted the top of her musical box. The faint melodic tone of *Come Back to Sorrento* filled the room. They both smiled and listened to the tune. By common consent the destination had to be Sorrento.

Suddenly Elizabeth's mood changed.

'What am I going to do about Michael?' she exclaimed.

'We'll tell him the same as we tell Julie and wait to see how he reacts.' he replied.

David's comment did not relieve the sudden panic she felt. All the joy that she experienced earlier in the day seemed to evaporate.

'David, I don't know how I am going to do this. I have to speak to my only son, not knowing how he will react.'

'Listen dear!' he replied. 'Your situation with Michael cannot get any worse than it is now. If he has any compassion, he should be able to accept what we are doing is for your own happiness.'

He could see that she was very upset and silently cursed the unreasonable nature of her son. He took her hand.

'Listen dear, let's leave this until tomorrow. We can start by fixing a date and then make the other arrangements. You go to bed, try to get a good night's sleep and I will phone in the morning.'

'You're right dear! Let's not spoil today.' she replied.

They walked to the front door and they kissed and lingered for a moment.

'Good night dear' she whispered.

David left the flat, got into his car and headed for home. He was worried for Elizabeth, knowing that all the earlier joy had drained away. He could only hope she would be in better spirits in the morning.

## Chapter Sixteen

## The Sands of Time

David found it very difficult to sleep for the first few hours. Too many thoughts about future events kept his brain from permitting sleep. Eventually he fell into a deep sleep until the shrill tone of his telephone sounded. He was startled and it took seconds before he was alert enough to recognise what was happening. His first thought was to look at the clock. It was three in the morning. Nobody rings at that time unless it is urgent so he jumped out of bed to pick up the receiver. Before he could answer, a very distressed voice had a message that would shatter his world.

'Mr Fulton, it's Grace here. Elizabeth's neighbour.'
Before he could get a word in she continued. 'It's about Elizabeth. She has just been taken to the hospital.'
He interrupted her. 'What has happened?'
'She wakened up about an hour ago and called me. She really sounded very unwell. I have her spare key so I went in to see her. She really was ill so I phoned for an ambulance and she has just left. She asked me to phone you and said you were not to worry.'

'Grace, thank you for looking after her and thanks for letting me know. You are a good friend and neighbour to Elizabeth. I expect she will be in the A&E ward so I will go there now and let you know what is happening.'

He dressed quickly, but he was in two minds about going to the hospital straight away. If she was in A&E he knew that he might have to wait some time before they would allow him to see her. He decided to wait for a while in the hope of finding her condition being assessed by then. There was no point in phoning the hospital, he knew they would not give any details. So he patiently waited until five in the morning when his patience deserted him. It was dark and the morning air had a chill that matched his concern.

When he arrived at the hospital the car park was nearly empty. He collected his parking ticket and made his way past two parked ambulances at the entrance to the A&E Department. A few people sat in the waiting room. Some were waiting to be attended and others were, like him, anxiously awaiting news of loved ones. He went straight to the enquiry desk and waited for someone to take notice and come to the desk.

'Can you give me any information about Mrs Stewart?' he enquired.
'First name?' Came the officious reply.
'Elizabeth, Elizabeth Stewart.'
'I think she is still waiting to be assessed as far as I know.'

Can I go in and see her?' he asked.

'Are you related?'

'No, I am her partner. We are not married, not yet.'

'That should be okay' she replied. 'I don't know which cubicle she is in, so go through these doors. Speak to the nurse at the desk and she will say if you can see her.'

The door opened into a long corridor Two ambulance crews were standing alongside patient trolleys waiting to transfer their patients into the hands of the hospital. He approached the desk and waited until a doctor and the nurse finished their conversation.

'Can I help you?' asked the nurse.

'Yes, can you give me any information about Elizabeth Stewart. I think she was admitted early this morning.'

The nurse checked her records before replying.

'She has been assessed and she will be transferred to a ward as soon as a bed becomes available.' The nurse gave him a cubicle number and advised him not to stay too long.

He drew back the curtain of the cubicle where Elizabeth was lying on a bed. She was sedated to ease her pain so she looked calm but very pale. She appeared to have aged since he last saw her just a few hours ago. He placed a chair beside her bed and held her hand. He tried to speak to her but his mumbled words were of little comfort. She recognised him and gave a weak smile. He sat beside her for ten minutes until a nurse came to say it was time for him to go. He rose from his chair, leaned over the bed and kissed her brow.

She whispered weakly. 'Tell Michael.'

Before leaving, he spoke to the nurse. 'Do you know which ward she will be in?'

'Best to phone reception after nine when they should know which beds have been vacated. At the moment all the wards are full.' she replied.

He now had to deal with Elizabeth's request. As promised he phoned early enough to catch him before he left home for work. He dialled Michael's number and waited for a reply, not knowing how he would be received. Michael was still at home and when he heard David's voice he sensed that this was something to do with his mother. So he listened with out any thought of being rude.

'Michael I am sorry but I have bad news for you. Your mother is in hospital and she is not very well.'

Michael took a few seconds to respond. 'What is wrong with her is it really bad?'

'I don't have any details yet. When I saw her this morning she was still in A&E waiting to be transferred to a ward. I am going to phone later this morning to get more details.' he replied.

'Do I need to come up to Southport to see her?'

'Look, I will give you the hospital number. You speak to them first before you decide.'

Elizabeth's request had been dealt with, now he had to find out which ward she was in and what was wrong with her. He waited until after nine before phoning the hospital. The receptionist gave him the ward number but could say nothing about her condition. He was transferred to the ward but all they would say was that she was sedated and comfortable. Without further delay he set off to the hospital, parked his car and collected his parking ticket. He walked along the main corridor of the hospital, following the overhead signs directing visitors to all the facilities provided by the hospital. The sign for her ward directed him upstairs to another corridor and to the entrance to the ward. The door was locked because it was outside visiting hours. He pushed the bell and with increasing apprehension waited for someone to allow him into the ward. After a few moments the door unlocked.

Elizabeth was in a single room. That pleased him because there was privacy and she was away from the many disturbances of the main ward. The door was open and his initial reaction was one of shock. She was flat on the bed and appeared to be coupled up to an array of medical apparatus. She looked uncomfortable and in a state of semi consciousness. He sat beside her and took her hand and tried to speak to her but she said nothing except to exchange a flickering eye contact. The visit was interrupted by the arrival of the nurse who asked him to wait outside to allow the house doctor to examine her.

While he was waiting outside the room he went to ask the staff nurse about Elizabeth's condition. She was reluctant at first because she did not recognise him as a near relative. He explained his position and the nurse relaxed when he told her about Michael and the need to keep him informed. She asked him to wait until the doctor finished his examination for him to explain her condition. Shortly after, the doctor left the room and the nurse introduced David to the doctor.

The doctor explained. 'Mrs Stewart is seriously ill. We believe she is suffering from a rare form of leukaemia which has reached a critical stage .This has put her heart under severe strain. If you are in contact with her next of kin you should advise them to visit her as soon as possible.'

David was distressed by this information. He knew from the doctor's comments that her life was in danger. The doctor was about to leave then he turned towards David.

'Perhaps you can help. I've been looking at Mrs Stewart's medical records and see that she has missed her last routine medical appointment. Do you know why?'

David was puzzled. 'No, she never mentioned that to me.'

The doctor then added, 'Before that there is no record of a blood test requested by her surgery.'

David was embarrassed by the depth of his ignorance and was unable to explain why she would do this and not mention it to him. The doctor's final words shattered him.

'It's a great pity she did not attend these appointments. The results would have given us vital time. I'm afraid we have lost that opportunity.'

Before leaving the hospital David called Michael and explained as best he could the seriousness of his mother's condition. He repeated the doctor's advice that he should attend his mother urgently. Michael confirmed that he was leaving home as early as possible next morning.

When David got home he realised he had been up for hours without food. He made a light breakfast, took it into the lounge and settled in his chair. He suddenly felt very tired but resisted the temptation to close his eyes. Then he began to think about the doctor's words. He wondered why she had missed her appointments. Was it his fault because she felt she would lose him because she was no longer attractive to him? Or, was it her decision to deliberately ignore the signs of her illness? He recalled her periodic spells of headaches, her tiredness and withdrawal. Were they the early undetected signs of her present perilous position? Or, heaven forbid. Was it because of the excitement she was exposed to yesterday? He was conscious of all these possibilities and was troubled by the same feeling of guilt that haunted him during his late wife's illness. In his heart he now knew that the clock could not be turned back.

## Chapter Seventeen

## The Last Reunion

David attended the afternoon and evening visiting hours. He tried to tell Elizabeth that Michael was on his way and thought he saw a slight flicker of recognition in her eyes. He prayed that her son would arrive soon because he saw in her the same signs he saw in his wife as her days neared the end. At the end of the evening visiting hour the nurse told him he could stay with Elizabeth longer. He was tired and had little to eat all day and he was deeply saddened by it all. He did not stay but drove home. Fully clothed, he lay down on his bed and fell into a troubled sleep.

The following morning he wakened up in a dream induced sweat. He was relieved that there was no night call from the hospital and he had the forlorn hope that her condition might have improved. Now his intention was to go back to Elizabeth as quickly as possible. Access to the ward was still restricted. He rang the bell and was admitted straight away. He enquired about Elizabeth and was told she was comfortable but her condition was still critical. It was unfair to ask the nurse about the possibility of some form of medical intervention so he decided to leave that question until he saw a doctor or a consultant.

David opened the door and saw that she was asleep. Her breathing was heavy and disturbed. He sat at the side of her bed and gently held her hand with the intention of remaining there for the rest of the day, and tomorrow if needs be.

It was afternoon and visitors were arriving to visit patients in the main wards. Lunch had passed him by and he had been sustained by the occasional cup of tea provided by the catering staff. He left her to go to the hospital restaurant for a hastily consumed lunch. When he returned Elizabeth was being attended to by two young nurses and a doctor was in deep discussion with the staff nurse. He remained outside the room until they had finished. Then he went forward to speak to the doctor.

'Excuse me, can you tell me anything about Mrs Stewart?'

The doctor excused himself from the nurse and ushered David to one side.

'Mrs Stewart is critically ill. The excess of white cells in her blood are putting her heart under severe strain. There is very little we can do at this late stage except to make her comfortable.'

He continued, 'I'm very sorry but you and her family need to prepare for the inevitable.'

'Is there no medical procedure available?' David asked.

The doctor hesitated. 'There comes a point in time when we all have to accept that the end of a life is inevitable,'

David's thoughts turned immediately to his wife Clare. That phrase 'the end of life' was engraved on his soul.

It was early evening and he was still sitting beside Elizabeth. Still holding her hand which felt cold but he could feel a slight pressure on his fingers. This was the only link he had with her as he tried to transfer some warmth into her silent body. Unexpectedly the door to her room opened and Michael stood there. He paused briefly to take in the sight of his mother with David alongside her. For a moment, David wondered how her son would react to his presence. He stood up and walked towards Michael. He stretched out a hand and was relieved when Michael acknowledged the gesture. They both relaxed as David pointed to his vacant seat. Michael moved towards his mother and kissed her brow. David placed a second chair on the other side of her bed and they sat there each holding her hand.

This was the first time Michael had seen his mother since she last visited him, when he tried but failed to persuade her to give up David. This was the first time the two men in her life met. The circumstances were so tragic that David felt that mother and son should be left alone. He rose from his chair, telling Michael that he would wait outside to give him some personal time alone with his dying mother.

He went outside and discussed Elizabeth's condition with the duty nurse. She was sympathetic but professional in the way that she spoke.

This reminded him of the same professional approach by the nurses who attended his wife when she was nearing the end of her life. It was the nature of their calling to be able to deal with personal tragedies without becoming too emotionally involved, to the detriment of their care.

His conversation stopped when Michael came out of the room and approached David.

'I think you should come back into the room. I think Mother would want you there.'

They both walked in together and sat either side of the bed, quietly holding her hands. Then David felt the slightest pressure on his fingers. They both looked at each other and knew they experienced the same sensation. Somewhere deep in her failing body she found the strength to unite her lost son and her beloved partner. This was the last act of her life. Her last breath came from deep down in her body and her gentle grip faded away.

Michael gazed at his mother's lifeless face and cried softly. David placed her outstretched arm under her bed sheet and sat in silence for a few moments. Then he left Michael alone with his mother to alert the medical staff, knowing that they would have to leave her in the hands of the hospital.

A few minutes later Michael left the room and placed a hand on David's arm.

'David.' he paused and then said.

'I want to thank you for making Mum's life so happy for the last few years. I owe you an apology. I was not the son she deserved. It's too late now so I hope you can forgive me on behalf of her?'

David was taken aback by Michael's confession. He put his arm around his shoulder, just like a father comforting a son.

'There is nothing to forgive. Your mother understood your feelings and carried the guilt knowing that she had lost you because of me.'

There were formalities to be completed at the hospital that Michael had to deal with. David stayed with him and when he was finished he spoke to him.

'You have a lot to do now to sort things out. Please let me help you, I know how difficult it is going to be.'

He took out his key ring and released his spare key for Elizabeth's flat and gave it to Michael.

'This is yours now. Why don't you go there this evening? It will be a start in getting to know what needs to be done and renewing memories of your Mum.'

Michael nodded in agreement.

David continued. 'I am going to phone your Mum's neighbour, she was a good friend and she will help you, I'm sure. So come on, let me drive you there.'

Michael was grateful for David's help. As they walked to the car park together he promised to keep in touch. It was comforting for David to know Elizabeth's memory would live on in the new found friendship of her son.

David did not mention that they were planning to get married. That would remain a secret known only to him but he had one last thing to say to Michael.

'It was your mother's great regret that when she found me she lost her son. Before she passed away today I know she found you again and because of that her last moments were peaceful.'

David parked his car in the garage. He opened the door and entered the dark hallway. It brought back the memory of the first day Elizabeth called with her ridiculous briefcase. Now he was mentally and physically exhausted as he climbed the stairs and entered his bedroom. He sat on the bed gazing round to see all the things that added the woman's touch. These were the things that reminded him of Elizabeth. He took from his jacket pocket the small gift wrapped engagement ring and placed it on the dressing table alongside her personal things.

He gazed at these things and sighed, I've been here before!

David did not sleep well that night. It was disturbed with wild and chaotic dreams none of which he could recollect when he awoke in the morning, except for one. He recalled the vision of a young boy writing at a desk and a young girl walking into the distance. Something made him think of the poem he wrote a long time ago. He remembered telling Elizabeth about it and how she wanted to read it, she never did read it, nor did Clare before her.

Later in the day he searched for the elusive poem and found it in an old wallet hidden amongst other personal documents. He opened the wallet and took out a discoloured piece of paper folded twice into a small square. Carefully unfolding it, he began to read very quietly.

He folded the paper and returned it to the wallet, thinking how fitting it was that this naive teenage poem written long ago to lament the loss of a girl called Moira was now a lament to the only two women in his life with whom he shared his first and last affair.

# THE POEM

*You shine upon me like a star,*
*A star that shines down from afar.*
*So far away and yet so real,*
*That the touch of your hand, I can almost feel.*

*Oh, what cruel fate was it that decreed,*
*That you and I and our love be freed.*
*No more to slumber in your arms so warm,*
*But to cry in pain with a heart that's torn.*

*Oh, were it that I could live last year,*
*For then I would be of far greater cheer.*
*I'd sing, I'd dance and laugh and shout,*
*For then I'd be happy without a doubt.*

*You gave me something dear and sweet,*
*That all the wealth in this world can't beat.*
*But life is cruel, this world is cruel,*
*And no more shall you listen to this poor fool.*